"Gleeful, menacing, intellectually   t,
mind-bending novella that's part sto

The Cabin at the End of the   b

"*Ethics* is another mind-wrecker from a living master of weird fiction.
Cisco's horrors are agonizingly beautiful."
            – Laird Barron, author of *Swift to Chase*

"The first time I read Michael Cisco's *Ethics*, I thought I didn't
understand. The second time I read it, I realized it had cracked open
a part of my heart that had long ago calcified. *Ethics* is an
extraordinary, deeply moving story about the vast river of life, and
those creatures who briefly rise above its waves in their painful and
wondrous awareness of birth, life, and death. It is an astonishing feat
of language, intellect, and imagination, proof that Cisco is operating
at a level unlike any other writer working today; proof of his
singular, staggering talent."
            – Livia Llewellyn, author of *Furnace*

Ethics

Ethics

by Michael Cisco

Lovecraft eZine press

PART ONE

Streaking over the earth, the songbird lifts itself up slightly and then, folding its wings, drops into a shallow swoop toward cover as a flash of lightning bursts and gutters, and then, virtually in the same moment, a thunderclap swats the bird to the ground. The bird's skull fractures, with a crack that sets its jaw awry, and the pain and shock of crashing is doubled and redoubled with the searing, sugary torture of the split bone. The blasted bird lies turned onto its side, stunned in the tall grass, still dry, though whipped by the wind, which has begun to stink.

Suffering is playing all around the bird like that stinking wind. Suddenly, she sees the fire. The dream is in the light, the gold and scarlet color, the almost inaudible sound it makes, the impossibly nimble dance it's doing in place, and in the way it swells, as if the bird were hurtling up to meet it and only it, unmoored among all the other fixed things the bird can see. The noise of the fire is like the song of an unfamiliar type of familiar animal. There's a humming, like a swarm of bees. There's snapping, like twigs, rustling, like dry leaves, but then none of these familiar noises are ever produced at once by the same thing, not in any organized way. The fire-thing must have its own organization, which is the reason it sings in the way it does, using the most unusual things for its voice. The coloring is strange, because the noises have no associations whatever with bright things, like sparkling water running; but then the ocean also sparkles, and it roars. Incandescent gold sparkled into ruby and sullen bloody scarlet, lacings of symmetrically tongued crimsons and carmines, luminously tawny and sun-glazed sand. The fire looms over her now like a tree growing out of nothing, the stinking, coiling brilliance in front of her seems to want to poison and devour her senses like a swarm of vicious insects, but it is mysteriously contained in itself, even as it fights to hatch itself out of its own shape. The songbird stares in awe at the coilings of towering scarlet monster rearing itself out of nothing, no roots, nothing but grass and the level ground, taking in its writhing shapelessness, its struggles within its bottomless shape, as if it were a huge poisoned animal convulsing and sick, vomiting itself. The fire, set by lightning, dancing inside its irregular footprint and throwing itself impetuously up, up. Now it channels itself along its length to heighten this leaf, standing bolt upright out of its spiny, whirling mass, while now that leaf shrinks back down and becomes a spine while the fire, both the whole thing and a sort of darting shootingness inside it, transfers its upward groping along an adjacent limb.

She stares with horror at the beaded lashings sliding along the dry stalks of the grass only inches away from her. She struggles, her skull flaring and crackling with every movement, her head heavy and ungainly with pain, pulling her down to knock it against the ground and fan the flames inside fracture's jagged edges. She watches helplessly as a feeble sticklike arm of the fire effortlessly encircles her. She is trapped inside the fire. She screams. Stares. Screams. Stares. She has no balance, can't get her wings out to fly. Then a chance contraction concentrates her will, lifting her onto her feet. Just then, a lazy flirt of wind dashes a scrap of flame directly onto her, and she catches fire, the flames sucking greedily at her neck and face. Her right eye puckers, chars, goes out. The bird flails wildly, battering herself against the ground, all her muscles spasming. She flails into a cool patch of damp mud.

The pain is so total that it almost forces her out of herself. Her right side is slathered with mud. The right side of her face and neck are smoking, but the flames are extinguished. With what remains of her sight, she turns to find the fire, in order to escape from it, and sees that there is a brownish hollow space among the flames, returning her gaze like an unexpected eye.

"This is Reason" it says.

Pain, terror, calling for help, heard by nobody. The bird feels inside herself the same manic raking of the wind and clouds, the same calculated frenzy of spreading and converting, burning, eating, growing, swelling, becoming greater and more terrible, battling back the extinguishing wind, the quenching water the clouds have started dropping down on it, the tranquil rage of the reason that is the fire's and hers. Some part of the world has gone wild, but it all makes sense, flapping in this corner of the grass. Fire rings the damp patch chance tossed her into. Between her and the flames there are the same uncanny thermal tremblings that the terrible gulls use to climb into the sky every day. Smaller, more tumultuous. Seeing them, her pain immediately opens her wings. She teeters, and her pain widens her stance, spreads her wings. A wider target for the fire, but her pain feels beneath her wings the tumbling of hot air, agitated by the fire. Her pain leaps, flapping only twice and then reaching desperately for the jets of smoke bursting from the tips of the flames. They boil up, scalding her body. She inverts and is tossed through the air, tumbling up the rising fire-breath like a dead leaf. The wind sheers across her path and her wings open. Down the wind's long, cooling ramp she skates, overshooting the toothed, golden extremity of the fire. She slaloms toward a copse of trees, like streaks of icy blackness, the opposites of the flames. For her, to spot a branch is to reach for it, and though she can only see through her left eye, she is able to home in on a long, slender branch and snatch a perch on it, all her speed gone.

When the fire flicked out its tongue at her and burned her, she thought she heard it telling her, "This is Reason."

The scourges of the fire flog at the ground, the wind, the grass, the air, the clouds, saying, "This is Reason." Flatly. The passion of the flames is beneath something higher in the flames, coolly thinking, ardently doing what must be done, what only can be done.

A guttering, lunar pulsation of light snaps across the gloom, whipping in space above the grass. Another songbird streaks into a clump of bushes. Almost at once comes the deafening sound – a rattling, clapping report that bursts on the remit of the already vanished light like an ancient and enormous tree trunk sprung out from the flash, toppling down, creaking and groaning. Like the crash of a fallen tree in the woods, the call of this disembodied explosion spreads through the trees, stretching and thinning, but reviving against stones and slopes. The trees soak up the noise and rend and sieve it through their branches that still move too calmly.

Holes like mouths or eyes open and close all over the fire. There is vacancy inside it, at once like the inside of an egg, and like the dark eye in a garishly feathered face. The flame spreads in a shattered canopy that bounces off the ground, squirrels around itself, scurries into the grass in countless snow white snakes as the center bubbles and mushrooms red. The reeking belch that returns forces the songbird to turn smarting away. Now look at red angles that flap into dissolving black bulbs of smoke against the lividly-seamed, overcast sky. Out of the howling of the fire comes a worldwide hush as the heavy part of the rain rolls over. The water pours from the sky and beats down the red. Heavy droplets and spray kick up from wet grass. She watches the rain batten on the fire, clubbing it down. The fire blackens, hemorrhages white steam, as the rain serenely tramples it into the charred excrement of burned grass and scorched dirt at its base. It's like seeing a huge tree rot away to nothing before her eyes, as if that obscenity had been nothing more than mist. Where did it come from? Where did it go?

Now the rain is pelting down. The last thing her right eye ever saw had been a wavering blur of blonde light whose touch was distilled pain that tugged and dabbed at her. Compressed down onto her feet, her dizzy head splitting, she splutters and coughs up what little food she has in her stomach. A heavy raindrop smashes her in the head, and nearly knocks her from her perch. She inches her way toward the sluicing trunk, fixes herself, goes completely still, afraid to make any movement at all for fear of aggravating the terrifying, persisting torment that's fastened on her and that only grows fiercer, causing her to shrink into herself even further. Hunger and fatigue are starting to work on her, but this pain overrules them and her, keeping her nailed to the spot, motionless. She thinks over and over of her eggs, not knowing what this means exactly. Her mate will look after the eggs – sees the nest untended, filling with rain, her eggs drowning in icy rainwater.

To return to the nest, she will have to cross the open spaces, exposed to hawks and falcons who have only to see her to kill her. Wings beat the air like drums. The wingbeat is a solid thump and the outstretch is a sharp rap and spreading into the glide is a quiet crash. She imagines the cuckoo flitting up to her untended nest, which induces despair, which throws her in the air. Though it feels like she's ripping her skull, she drags herself up into the air again and again, plunging down in darting swings, driven toward the ground by the rain and forced to flap her wings violently to stay aloft, straining with all her will through her one eye to reach the next clump of covering trees, but she falters, shifts her vision lock to a big solitary bush well away from the trees. Clumsily she collides with its yielding branches and finds a purchase on a twig with one foot, everything in her head yawing violently back and forth. Now she stands on the twig, dripping rainwater. She drinks a little, sickening and cool. It sits inside her without mixing into her substance at all, and in a moment she coughs it back out again. She will have to work her wings a great deal to get up from down here. Nearly beaten down to the ground by the rain and wind, flapping crazily she gets up into the air and careens into the cover of the clump of trees, into a gloom composed of vertical strips of blue, grey, and brown hazes deepening into damp indigo, cold lead, saturated umber.

The next open space is so wide she has to cross it in three flights, stopping on the ground. Once she's safely under cover the woods, exhausted, she sits half buried in leaves, calling. A single, clear cry, over and over, dropping quickly at the end each time like a statement.

Somehow she makes her way to the tree where her nest is hidden. Feeble, clumsy flights. Dazed stumbling. One side of her head seems to be tearing off, excruciatingly slowly. She sits at the base of the tree for a long time, unable to gather the strength to fly up to the nest, but then she does it, contracting and then exploding, clambering up the air to the nest and perching on it, trying to look at the two eggs sitting there. She settles herself on them. She sits on them, as still as if she were dead, and her cruel pain becomes not entirely all of her.

Through the pain comes the fire's glorious memory, almost like a distinction of some kind bestowed especially on her. It throbs and trembles inside her like a blob of dew on a leaf, tumbling orange, incandescent copper and vermilion, explaining to her with godlike patience that it is the reason that the world resounds with, in a neverending recitation and elaboration of the Ethics, which cannot be heard in the same way as she would hear a sound, but which sounds in all sounds, is shown in all sights, is present at all times in all things and actions, through the stillest night time like a murmur of water just below the topsoil, but for all that in accents so powerful they turn the silence into something emphatic that does not so much shock the world as create it complete, all at once, like the burst of lightning throws a whole landscape at the eye at once. In her delirium, she thinks the Ethics bellows in the brightest and most raucous daylight, screams in the tumult of stormy wind, tickles heavy boulders and sways their bases, so that the scrape and parting of one crumb of earth from another happens just as one proposition follows another, according to the definitions and axioms.

"The mind is capable of perceiving a great number of things, and is so in proportion as its body is capable of receiving a great number of impressions."

Her body is receiving intolerable, lustrous pain that cries out for something she can't provide, relief or action, something, but she has to sit on her eggs, she must to sit still, or else half her head will scrape off along a white-hot fissure and its shards will drop like bits of eggshell to scatter among the roots below.

Under the direction of her delirium, she begins with the definitions ... one ... what hatches creates an echo, a kind of echo, beginning before singing, before there is a voice, and it is that which resonates already within the living egg ... two ... any thing that is gestating is considered to be a living egg, that is, within a shell ... to be gestating is preparation for singing, for any calling entity ... for example, a body is considered to be finite because we can always conceive of its hatching out into a new and still developing singer ... so, too, a thought hatches another thought ... but the singing body is thinking, and the song of thought starts out as a body ... three ... scintillation is that which is no longer itself, but which broods and hatches itself ... that is, that the gestation of which requires the conception of another thing from which it has receded like echoes of singing ... four ... thinking about scintillation is accompanied by phrasings ... drop to drop, the point, then distinction ... the refinement of the mineral, the subtraction of, the division of, the joining of, note to note, and rest to rest ... torment of steady work without motion, as the terms begin to knit, braided back into song from sound ... five ... mood is the kind of scintillation, that is, the particular way in which something hatches into something else ... six ... teemingness is the shadow, moonlight, or night remembrance of day, that is, the image of scintillation, consisting of any hatching which is free to compose and create echoes, to resonate without ending ... seven ... a thing that echoes in all directions, and is expected to act by teeming, is free ... a thing is considered to be unhatched or unfledged if it exists and acts in a faltering and uncertain way ... eight ... eight ... *eight* ... neverendingness is expressed in the echo, and means scintillation itself, insofar as it is conceived as freely following solely from the regularity of a neverending echo ...

The eight definitions wander in and out of a dreamless, half-smothered sleep of phantasmal browns and oranges, cooled by the rushing sound of rain splashing in the branches, piloted by the misery of healing that gushes through the fracture like lava channelled by rocky crags, down a night escarpment like a ribbon of liquid daylight. Will thoughts be guided? The eight definitions have to hold still in order to keep the environment from throwing up again, or tossing itself apart. Reason is guided against the sleep, and the upright sides of the escarpment of thought in the channels that water the definitions. Shallow rain channels cut the air and then vanish. The rain pulses down arteries hung in space, and axioms are what mark the course that reason takes to … to rewater the clouds, and cause the shower, the fullness of the downpour.

The definitions scream for axioms. A nest of hatchlings screams for food. There is a screaming for food underneath the misery contracted into a trickling seam high in the trees. The axioms come in their own time, falling one by one into the hunger like water, which fills the stomach without satisfying the hunger.

First axiom … all things hatch into the outside …

The separation of stomach and food. The drastic separation of stomach and food. The separation of the bird from its clutch of eggs, in order to put food each in the separated stomachs, is inevitable.

first … first axiom … all things hatch into the outside … second axiom … what cannot be hatched itself must be brooded … third axiom … hatching follows from brooding, and the chick follows from the egg, and the egg follows from the nest … and all things live this way …

The effect is to continue to sit on the eggs. It is necessary to stop sitting on the eggs. In order to go on sitting on the eggs it is necessary to stop temporarily. In order to avoid being killed by vomiting, it is necessary to put something new in the stomach. In order to repair the broken bone, and to heal the roasted skin and flesh, it is necessary to eat what these injuries will induce to be vomited, which entails moving, which will exacerbate these injuries and retard the healing. It is necessary to heal to end the suffering, but the suffering is healing.

fourth axiom … the knowledge of a brooding depends exclusively on the knowledge of a hatching … fifth axiom … only things which have nothing in common with each other can recede through each other … that is, the receding of the song does not involve the receding of the trees, the sounds heard through the shell have nothing in common with the egg …

The cry for help recedes unanswered into the striped blue and indigo, grey and brown. The pink light stands empty among the trunks and no help comes. The cry will never stop receding into a vacancy that grows ever greater to swallow it. The cry for help falls into the growling stomach of space.

sixth axiom … a true conception must hatch with any and all broodings … seventh … axiom … if an egg can be conceived as not hatching, then it is an echo, rather than a song …

The cry comes back at the same time that it recedes. The cry is not an answering promise of help. It is only the consciousness of suffering, its necessity made shining and unmistakable. There is no help. There has been some accident – a necessary one – and the songbird's mate is gone.

The misery of healing, the eggs, the hunger, the definitions, the axioms, the listening, intensified now that she cannot see on the right side. The heartbeat. The calls of scrub jays. The calls of crows. The calls of grouse. The breathing. The long-riding whisper of the trees. The crash of surf in the distance. The plunks and hiccups of the stream, mumbling over rocks. The regular call of dogs. The meshed calls of other songbirds. The calls of mourning doves. The calls of snipes. The calling of crickets. Axioms guide definitions. Among them appear inexorable propositions, with a regularity that is supernally indifferent, seeming now as if they were being articulated out of the elements of a flexible, boundless rhythm that burns all around her, and above, and below, and inside, and seeming now as if they were outshouting and burning through that rhythm.

apply the axioms to the definitions ... in the pouring rain ... in the frigid waterfall ... the pulsation of the heart in that cold blue curtain ... one ... scintillation is by nature simultaneous with all hatchings ... two ... scintillation has nothing else in common with itself ... three ... only the layer can be the cause of the egg, that is, the layer and the egg are not the same, and this is necessary ... the calls of the scrub jays, the pulsing of my heart ... four ... two or more distinct chicks are distinguished from one another by their calls ... five ... scintillation can only exist in the landscape ... six ... scintillation can only be caused by what is not scintillation ... seven ... the echo belongs to the nature of scintillation ... eight ... scintillation is free ... nine ... the more echo through the shell, the more it recedes ... ten ... the calls of crows, of grouse, my breathing ... my heart pounding ... each hatching of scintillation must be conceived through its receding ... eleven ... the echo of scintillation consisting of free phrasings is also free ... twelve ... no phrasing of scintillation itself can be truly hatched, from which it would follow that scintillation consists only in more laying ... twelve ... no, thirteen ... free scintillation is neverending recedingness of the mother's voice ... pounding ... pounding ... calling ... the crashing of surf ... the whisper of trees, droplets in trees ... gasping for breath ... breath to explain ... fourteen

... there can be, or be conceived, only other scintillations ... fifteen ... whatever is, recedes, and nothing can be layed or hatched without receding ... sixteen ... from the freedom in the air there must follow free travel in free ways ... that is, everything that can be produced by a mother's voice, freely echoing ... seventeen ... scintillation acts solely against the confines of its hatching, and hatches only to lay ... eighteen ... resonation of the mother's voice through the shell is the transitive cause of all things ... nineteen ... continue ... nineteen ... scintillation is neverending, that is, all of the phrasings of teemingness are neverendingly hatching ... twenty ... the echo of teemingness and the hatchings of the newborns are one and the same ... twenty-one ... all eggs that hatch from the absolute receding of teemingness have no mother... that is, through the receding, they are free songs ... the plunks and hiccups of the stream tumbling over rocks ... the calls of the ... the songbirds ... my thrashing heart ... my weary breathing ... this is what is general ... whatever ... twenty-two ... whatever follows from some phrasing of a mother exists freely, ie, as an echo ... twenty-three ... every mother's song which exists freely and full-fledgedly must have freely followed either from the absolute nature of some phrasing of a song or from some phrasing modified by a modification which is free and full-fledged ... twenty-four ... straining for air ... twenty four ... the essence of eggs layed by the singing of the mother invariably requires that they be beneath her body ... twenty-five ... the echo through the shell is the efficient cause not only of the hatching of things but also of their avian phantomishness ... the mourning doves ... the snipes ... the crickets and songbirds ... my heartbeat ... my choked breathing ... twenty-six ... what acts as expected is expected by teemingness ... continue ... twenty-seven ... a thing which has been expected by teemingness to act in a particular way remains surprising ... twenty-eight ... every individual thing must be under the body of its mother ... twenty-nine ... everything is surprising, like the precise appearance of the newborn, but all things are from the free teeming of scintillation, surprising to recede, surprising to approach ... the convulsing heart, the barking dogs, rain falls harder, breath coming shorter ... the father's song is always surprising ... thirty ... the finite voice in action must comprehend the phrasings of teemingness and the recedings of teemingness, as well as everything else ... thirty-one ... the voice in singing or calling, whether hatched or no, must be related to the song singing, not to the song sung ... thirty-one ... no ... two ... thirty-two ... song cannot be called a free cause, but only a surprising effect ... the father is always willful ... thirty-three ... things could only have been hatched by teemingness in any other way or in any other order than is the case ... thirty-four ... is it thirty ... thirty-four? ... thirty-four ... songs are haunted by their very power ... thirty-five ... whatever we conceive to be within the song's power, the song will accomplish ... thirty-six ... nothing ... nothing ... nothing exists from whose receding a brooding does not ... does not follow ...

"This is reason."

The woods skirt low hills and roll with the land toward the ocean, breaking up into isolated copses on its way down into the open grass, softened and greened by fog. The air above the treetops whips in flashing, sunny reversals of wind; the birds who fly that high are adept at turning right angles. As the day waxes, thermal columns rise perpendicularly from exposed patches of heated rock, turning them into the bases of huge pillars of roiling, air-buoyed gulls, kites, shearwaters, steadily aloft, screwing them into the boughs of the middle air. They soar well above the tops of the lawned hills, where oaks with heads of glittering froth and wandering trunks grow in isolation like wooden thermals, scaled by squirrels, beetles, ant columns, caterpillars. Bolted together by oak roots, the hills seem at once to grow and subside just sitting there, as if they weren't folds of the landscape but lumps from some sky pressing the earth like feet in bushy, green felt clogs. Far in back of them stand black mountains, still guanoed with snow and trapping the clouds in their flight inland from the scooting plovers of the shore. They rise and drive back the clouds toward the ocean, which keeps whipping up more spray, and the land in between buckles, sprouting blackhead trees from its pores, and cracking in gullies where white rivulets dart through a crease and then splay out tumbling into countless shallow reflecting pools glimmering in divots set deep as jewels in scored black clay and bright green grass. All over the open ground and in among the trees as well, these pools are cataracted eyes pushed like glass fakes into the soil, with strawberries poking from their corners.

A narrow strip of grey-brown sand fringed with iron rocks separates the thinning grassy slope from the endless blasts of dead green-and-white wind and seawater curling against and goading each other to slump down onto the flattened beach again and again, with roars. At dawn everything down here is smeared with rose and violet, the shingle glows, and a gigantic spirit of color lifts out of the rocks and water, rises in the air and pulls all the other colors up, then splits and subsides further upward, above the highest fliers. The sun for that day flies straight toward the ocean, over it toward the shore, then flies past and disappears behind the mountains, never to return, but to be followed by another just like it. An endless one-way migration of strictly solitary fliers, no one can follow it any more. It must be where they go to die, shyly invisible behind that rock wall. The shore blanches as each sun drops toward the mountains, although now the sky is completely bare of clouds and uncanny with peach and powdery blue, like the inside of an eye whose iris is the ocean and whose pupil is the ground, all dirty, clogged with rocks and trees. The day dawns, and with the air-change and the light-shaftings the songbirds have to respond with singing. The males show themselves and sing. "This is reason."

The air sluices through the trees, and at night it gathers itself together, and in the morning it slides gradually back into motion, contracting into tight points that clatter over the body like flakes of ice. The air off the water sounds with a heavy rumbling tone that carries a sense with it of diffuse warning, and from time to time, especially as it strikes the resonator of the woods, that tone becomes a continuous bass melody underscoring the motion of leaves, branches, and litter with a doomed feeling. Even then, there is a lighter, celestial chord that sweeps in from space, almost chiming, exciting the ear sensually, at once caressing and rough, eerie and reassuring, like the distant conversing voices of cloud tops. While the wind that races down from night is like the freshets of a black overflow, clear and colorlessly dark, shoring up night's darkness, stirring it and distributing its countless fragrances along triangular courses.

*

The smaller of the songbird's two chicks fell from the nest and died only days after he hatched. The remaining chick was large and vigorous and ate enough for two, so that, without her mate to help her, the songbird had to spend all day searching for food, from the moment his screams of hunger dragged her from sleep before dawn to final ebbing out of daylight. Her one good eye did not fail to notice the corpse of the other chick, crumpled and battered at the base of the tree, although she had not been present to witness the larger chick trampling it, then driving it furiously over the edge of the nest to fall to its death. With her altered vision, she didn't notice that her one remaining chick bore less and less resemblance to either her or her mate with every passing day, any more than she noticed the minor fungal infection pearling the ruined socket of her right eye.

The infection develops, the fractured skull knits, burned flesh scars over, the cuckoo chick burgeons, the songbird exhausts herself to feed it while her dead chick melts into the ground, axioms form and branch in lemmas, channel postulates like rain –

Axiom I: Bodies are either moving or not moving.
Axiom II: Moving bodies move at different speeds.

> Lemma I: Bodies are told apart by their speeds, and by whether or not they move, and not in any other way.
> Lemma II: This is true of all bodies.
> Lemma III: Bodies are moved by each other.

Postulates:
> First, bodies have parts.
> Second, some parts are hard, some soft, some wet, some dry. Some are further inside than others.
> Third, bodies are vulnerable to other bodies.
> Fourth, bodies depend on other bodies.
> Fifth, when one body causes another body's fluids to press on the soft parts of the body, it changes that body's shape and leaves a mark.
> Sixth, bodies can act on, move, and displace other bodies.

Listening for the moment to add her singing to the song all around her. Sing, turn head, listen. Watch. Not watching for anything, just watching. Listen. Then, when the moment comes, sing. How do you know the moment has come? Because you sing. So the listening becomes singing, while remaining listening. And when she stops singing, she's still singing, because she's listening to sing again. So the moment comes, and she sings, but not because she has decided that the moment has come. There is no wrong moment.

Very little remains of her past. She remembers a weary, familiar-smelling form that came and went, thrusting food down her throat, or gathering her and the others closer together, sharing the warmth and reassuring weight of a body, with the rain trickling down its sides, and she remembers singing, rising up in between the piercing cries for food. Those cries all around her had been maddening, at once goading her to raise her voice louder and louder until she was more weary from crying than from hunger, a kind of madness of a group, and at the same time those cries were not distinct from hers, and formed a crowd she could safely lose herself in. A cacophony that stung her ears, so that it was a relief when the pitch began to drop, when vision and other senses developed around that howling orifice and made it possible to become interested in other things, weakening her hearing as her other senses developed, multiplying her attention as well as dividing it, and a crazymaking sound, by turns depressing and infuriating. She'd had one especially large nest mate who had outbellowed all of them, and more than once had nearly kicked her up over the edge and out altogether, but she had struggled and even pecked until the message got through. Through that din she had managed to catch, from time to time, the robust, lively, complicated song of a male, and it stirred up in her an appetite that was subtle and vague. The impulse was still shapeless; the only direction it knew was up, that is, toward awareness, a contour that could be known, as well as toward power to act. This curious line connected that singing to her body's transformation as she grew, fledged, began to fly. As a female bird she would not be required to sing, but she still had to know the songs of the males; she didn't have to learn to sing those songs, but how to have those songs sung to her. If she hadn't known how, she would not have been able to satisfy the urge to breed and lay eggs that crystallized ever more distinctly in her. The male sings about his own body and everything he can do. His song gives you all of himself first, so your mate first exists for you as a song. Among all the endless singing, each is individual and plainly discernible from all the others, so a mistake in identifying singer and song is virtually unheard of. At the same time, the song declares nothing but itself. It is all the music there is, or there is none. It starts out complete, then unravels. It does not unfold in time. The song exists in time, but excuses both the singer and the listener from successive moments. The singing becomes a brief new world for the singer and the listener. The moment a female bird becomes a listener to a particular male's song, the selection has already been made, and the song is the music of that selection. On and on it goes, deepening the selection. The male has already chosen the one to come, and when the song conjures her up like a spirit answering a spell, he is already hers. But the singing doesn't stop there, or even after the eggs are laid and hatched. The males keep singing, and perhaps they consider themselves to be singing for some other reason, but, to her, her father's song cinched her in place every bit as much as did the nest and the brooding weight of her harried, easily-flustered mother. That is, since the song she heard cinched her in place, she assumed it was her father's song, since it fulfilled a role for her that formed an essential complement to her mother's care; it was a father's song as far as she was concerned, whoever was doing the singing. But how could a song affect her so much, drawing her up toward life, like a sun draws heliotrope, if it didn't give her that male bird, and if she didn't have some of his make-up in herself? She never saw him knowingly, which was not unusual; there were many possible fathers around, and she never heard any of them sing. On one occasion, she had heard the song she considered her father's, and quickly investigating, found all of the neighborhood songbirds flocked together in a tree – so many of them she couldn't tell if any of the possible fathers, or if all of them, were in it. It wasn't long before she forgot all about fathers and mothers, though, since it was on that occasion that she met her mate.

The wind blows, the bough bobs up and down with her riding on it. The wind smooths everything around. There's a salt ocean smell for a moment. A hieroglyph opens, and darts its lances and blanks into time. The phrases lengthen and the pauses grow deeper; they stretch like membranes. Dread gaps that pounce and choke off aphoristic phrases whose completion comes as a surprise, an eager silence welling up. Calling with the splits between the trees and branches, above the rocks, the sound carries across the stream tumored with a pool, scum-lidded and froth-spiralled. The phrases are twists and beams. Out come flashes of bright sound, pure tones from all songs, knocks and bangs from a haunting, the sighing and trilling of breath and air, the sound of snow falling, the sound clouds make when the gleaming magenta winks out and they turn blue, the nostalgic sound of the angles and curves recoiling from the mountains, their ominous stillness, their colors.

*

Something alien in the tone drags these sounds. They all have a shattered quality. The sounds are like puzzle rock, which seems complete but disassembles into dust and shards under any pressure. The shape of the sound, which is nothing, not even a bubble, holds together its tones. This is accomplished by the relationship of the sounds and pauses to each other, so, just like puzzle rock, the mass altogether holds the internal shapes.

"Did you hear it?" the plover asks her. "It was strange singing. I've just heard it now. Where is it? Did you hear it, too?"

"Do you hear it now?"

"No, not now. It was strange. In part, it was strange because it sounded like you."

"Perhaps it was me. I was singing just a moment ago."

"Females don't sing," the plover says. "You're female. Females don't sing."

"I do sing. That was probably my voice you heard just now."

"Demonstrate for me. I don't know what you mean."

At this request, the songbird, although she is hoarse and exhausted from singing, resumes her song, listening, singing, turning her head, waiting, singing. But the plover doesn't seem to understand.

"What? That? What was that?"

"Was that what you heard?"

"I'm not sure. Yes, well, a bit like it, but also not like it. It had a more far-away sound before."

"You were farther away before."

"Yes, well, but that isn't exactly it, I mean, not simply that it was far away from me, but that, even as I came toward it, since I was, as it were, compelled to investigate such a bizarre noise, it kind of kept its distance, and wouldn't exactly allow me to hear it directly, straight on."

"That was me, singing."

"Females don't sing, you know that. You're female."

"Yes, I know I'm female. But I have a voice, anyway, so I may sing."

"I thought you had a voice so that you could *call*, not sing."

The plover raises its head as high as it will go, tilting its beak straight up toward the sky, evidently thinking. Then, as if it had only been stretching, it abruptly lowers its head.

"I wasn't calling, I was singing," the songbird says.

"It didn't sound much like singing to me."

"You called it singing."

"When?"

"Just now."

"Ah, I must have been listening to something else," the plover says coyly.

"Anyway, there's nothing wrong with my singing if I want to."

"I don't think you should."

"If I have a voice, shouldn't I sing?"

"You might try a little singing now and then, I do that myself, to tell the truth, we all do. Although really you should only use your voice to call, not to sing. Males sing. You're female. But we do all sing, rarely. But not that way."

"I want to keep singing. I want to keep singing that way."

"Why that way?"

"Because that's the way it comes out."

"It's barely singing at all. I wouldn't call it singing, if I were you."

"Then perhaps I'm not singing, but making some other kind of song. Noise."

"If it's a song, then you're singing."

"Then I'm singing."

"You aren't calling either."

"No, it's more like answering."

"What are you answering?"

"I don't know, but I wouldn't do it for no reason, so there must be a reason."

The songbird is getting worked up, and now she is so tired she has to lean against the trunk of the tree.

"The Ethics says that the highest good is to live in harmony with others."

"I agree of course," the songbird says, a little impatiently, not so much with the conversation, or with the plover, as with her own fatigue, which seems to have permanently joined itself to her, becoming her primary characteristic.

"And you call *that* harmonious?"

"I don't know, it may be."

"It is harmonious to recede from those who aren't harmonious themselves."

"I suppose, but the Ethics says that the highest good is to live in harmony with others."

"I just said that! Are you falling asleep?"

"No, if only I were! But the Ethics says the highest good is to *live* in harmony with others. To live, you see."

The plover resettles its two feet before it responds.

"I don't follow you."

"I can't seem to live without it. Without singing, I mean. Trying to sing."

"Why not?"

"Songbird."

"Female songbird. Females don't sing. But they do live. – What happened to your eye?!"

"A fire."

"A fire!?"

More than astonishment, this explanation seems to make the plover almost indignant. Yet the shocking mental impression of the moment, the vivid presentiment of agony, the irredeemable loss of an eye, stymies the plover. Its gaze hovers somewhere about the songbird's feet, fixed and unblinking, its beak opening slightly, then closing again.

"A fire!" it says at last, unable to accept the idea that the songbird, after having been blinded in a fire, is able to conduct an ordinary conversation.

"You are singing – trying to sing –" the plover corrects itself, "– *because* the fire burned you."

As the songbird appears to think this over, the cuckoo's voice suddenly resounds in the air, swelling from the thickest part of the woods. The songbird dwindles. The plover cocks its head to listen. The call has its own shadow of quiet.

"Creepy, these woods," the plover says.

*

The cuckoo has a sly, contemptuous expressionlessness in its face. Behind it, there are sprawling, massive, naked chicks, with dull red bodies and heads like smooth black pebbles, covered in a goose-pimples, ungainly, wallowing in a stranger's nest, the forest floor below littered with the remains of the other chicks.

The cuckoo's call is a mocking riddle, mercilessly repeated in gentle tones.

how do?
you know?
your young?
your own?

*

There is something about the cry of her one remaining chick that grates on her; a hacking noise at the back of the throat that lends an air of angry impatience to its shrieking for food. This chick is now so large it is nearly threatening; larger than the songbird herself, but its impotence only swells on all the food she wearily drags back to the nest. When she feeds it, its gaping mouth nearly engulfs her whole head, her face is entirely within its convulsing throat. She searches her memory, unable to recall whether or not she has ever had any chicks before. It seems to her she has, but this vague impression is all that arises in response to her summons. Perhaps those were dreams, and this is the first time? She is certain that it isn't, but she it's a certainty she can't account for in any way.

The songbird perches on a branch with her one good eye on the nest. Inside it, she can hear the chick heave itself into a new position, trying to find the most comfortable posture for screaming. Those screams will send her darting off into space once more – she can't help it.

The song of every mood must involve the nature of the body and also the nature of the external body singing.

If the body is affected in a manner which involves the nature of any external body, the mind will regard that external body as actually existing, until the mind be affected in such a way, as to exclude the existence or the presence of the said external body.

If the body has once been affected by two or more bodies at once, then, when the singer afterwards sings any of them, it will straightway remember the others also.

The song in the mind is also in scintillation, following in scintillation in the same manner, and being referred to scintillation in the same manner, as the song of the body.

The singer does not know itself, except in so far as it perceives that the modifications of the body are modifications of the song.

The knowledge of the neverending echo of scintillation which is the burden of every song is adequate and perfect.

The singer is determined to wish this or that by a cause, which has also been determined by another cause, and this last by another cause, and so neverendingly on.

The chick's head wobbles feebly up over the edge of the nest. Its eyes are black, greasy slits thinly filmed over with transparent flesh. The edges of the beaked mouth part, spread wide, and from the depths of its hollow insides, raw and pulpy as sundered fruit, comes a rasping, penetrating scream of hunger that is repeated over and over again like an insult, straight up into the air. At the sound, the songbird flits away through the trees, her aching joints grinding against each other, the air forced in and out of her lungs violently by her almost panicked wingbeats, straining her one remaining eye to probe the darkness for more food, the dartings and seethings of more food.

When next she can rest, when her massive chick has fallen asleep, lying limp on its face like a corpse, its ragged red mouth still a little agape, the songbird can only sleep uncertainly herself. Expecting the imperious command for more food at any moment, she is jolted awake by the least noise. She seems already to hear her chick's voice, screeching. There is something wrong with that sound, she thinks, but without being able to determine what it is. She believes the sound ought to remind her of ... something – but her chick is totally unfamiliar in both sound and appearance.

There is nothing all that surprising or interesting in that, she thinks. Why should I assume that every chick will be the same? Why should a chick resemble either of its parents?

That thought strikes her insides with a sensation of intense cold.

Why should that thought be so startling? Why does it feel this dangerous to think like that?

When next her chick cries, she will immediately bestir herself to feed it, no matter what.

But what could induce her to do differently? Why should that be something she would need to tell herself she will do?

The thoughts waver in and out, like heavy flies, clumsy, loud, slow, swinging through space waiting for some reason to land, or sitting in place, stupefied, then streak away, no reason. Round and round, searching, but for nothing. Mindlessly roaming. Stupid. Back and forth. Stop. Go. It scrapes its eyes, then sits in a daze, then scrapes its unseeing eyes again. Airborne dirtclods trailing crumbs of curdled soil and saliva, and buzzing with the sleepy noise of idiocy as they bump against trees and stones. Flick one out of midair and ram it down a screaming, jelly-red throat, like a packet of silence that a bottomless hunger will dissolve entirely in a moment or two. Collect stupidities one by one, drag them heavily back to the nest, stuff them in a swollen, raging stomach, this chick of hers, now horrid with its first feathers. Soon it will leave, she reassures herself, and she will be free of it at last.

It will never leave, she thinks in despair, and the idea makes her want to crumble. Her injuries, her slowly healing bones, her aching muscles and sore feet, the fatigue that makes her more dead than alive, all loom up suddenly like idols of clear ice in the darkness, and demand she make herself nothing more than them. Stuff the chick with flies, black, oily, and stinking, buzzing with fury, stuff the bugs down the gullet, jelly-red, call out to the mate you now know is dead, stagger, fly, hunt, return, in sleep and in waking the same, feed it the same, but never the other, never any other, not like any other this one, so much larger, so much louder, so much more hideous, so greedy and sullen, face at rest like a monster too tired to complain for the moment, and not like the other, never the others, not there, not even a little, not herself, not her mate, flew away into a huge thick-gutted monster that overflows the nest and can barely raise its massive head, except to shriek deafeningly for food, food, food, stuff me with black foulness, stuff your aching half broken head down my throat –

Nothing can be destroyed except by a cause external to itself …

The chick emerges from the egg –

Things cannot co-exist in the same larger thing, insofar as one is capable of destroying the other … – and the egg from the mother and now the mother is going to vanish down the throat of the chick –

The singer sings those things which increase or help the power of activity in the body … booming with screams like a hollow log, but not the other, no, HERS. The monster! HERS. Fly, stare, peck the fly from the air – When the singer sings things which diminish or hinder the body's power of activity, it endeavors, as far as possible, to remember things which exclude the existence of those hindering things … bring it back and give it to it, it – it – HER chick. HERS – Hence it follows that the singer shrinks from conceiving those things which diminish or constrain the power of itself and of the body … So much larger than she is – than her mate ever was, than any of their kind, so-called, ever were, but HERS. A freak, must be. HERS. HERS!

What happened? She was flying, yes. She fell, somehow, not knowing how nor ever knowing how, the sickening crack of her head on the ground and the ensuing gusher of pain – the fire! She burned – she was blinded in her right eye – searing agony – the fire somehow stops – she's trapped, but sees the thermals, rises on them, is flung clear. All this was, it has happened, it is not happening now, it's over, entirely over. She returned to that surviving chick – HERS – HER surviving chick.

*

Dusk, to her, is the moment when all the world's colors invert, their daylight luster giving way to an ember-like, nocturnal fluorescence. Green becomes black, yellow is silver, blue is invisible, orange amethyst, and red deepens to a sulfurous brown. Movements at night are swathes of smeared outlines, like stains that glimmer back into the shade gradually. The purring of crickets and the flounce of wind through the bracken is probed, now and then, by the smothered hooting of an eagle owl, that once struck the songbird as both menacing and sorrowful, like a sobbed threat. Now, when she hears the eagle owl, she has the insane impulse to answer it. She might see it coming, but she would hear nothing. The owl's call means the owl is present, but not hunting. The owl's silent presence is the real danger. Tonight she notices the straining way the owl hoots; it must have to push hard to get its throat to create that sound, so unlike her own voice, which bounds out of her almost of its own accord, each distinct sound leaping aloft like a grasshopper. The owl doesn't raise its head and project its call, it puffs itself up on its perch and squeezes the noise out with the same expression of impersonal ferocity that it always wears, as if it were self-conscious, and a little embarrassed. The owl is not terrible when it calls, but only when that fierce face looms up out of the darkness in perfect silence, the eyes suffused with perfect concentration and expanding like the sky.

She wants to call to it, but it will stop hooting and start hunting soon anyway and, although that is a threat to her life, the songbird sees in her mind the owl standing over a limp form of the cuckoo, tearing at it through its feathers and bolting down shreds of its meat, pausing to glance confidently around before ripping another piece of flesh free, and the vision is so bitterly satisfying that it somehow leavens her fear and awakes a feeling of anger as savage and yet remote as the violence of a distant storm. Although her whole body is limp with fatigue, that chaotic feeling throws her into the air again. She flies from branch to branch, her body throbs with her breathing, going to the owl.

Swimming wildly into the night she ploughs right into smoke-thickened air; amber flickers up, brilliant in a black cage of brambles off to her right. Without a thought, she aims for it. Human voices bring her up short and she stops abruptly, alighting on a high bough overlooking the small clearing. Three gargantuas are moving in inexplicable ways around the fire, which erupts in a small but fierce blaze hemmed in by stones. One of the giants prods it with a stick. Bright motes wriggle up from the flames and twist away, half hidden in the foul belt of smoke that scrabbles into the treetops.

What is this a sign of?

Fire is not a thing like a stone or a tree. It's more like wind, streamingness, but the fire is more like a tree than the wind in that it has a shape, perhaps like the shape of a tree tossed by the wind, not as constant as a rock, but not shapeless like a wind. Like a rock, it doesn't divide, but doubles. A split rock becomes two rocks. A split fire becomes two fires. But the fire will grow, and the rock can only shrink. Rocks don't vanish altogether out of sight, and neither do trees. A fire can wink out of existence, and it can spring up fully formed out of nothing. It grows and moves and eats like a living thing, but crazy, so much faster, and living things don't give off light, and aren't conjured from nothing and into nothing, with no bones, no skin, no face. It's like life running away with itself, forgetting all about shape, with no predators or limits, but what life is destroyed by water? What life leaves no corpse?

The fungal infection makes her burned out eye socket look as if it were half-packed with cotton wool. The wind tugs at its fibers. A spark catches in a projecting white tuft. It blackens, and a thin streak of smoke etches the air past the songbird's head. Then the wind extinguishes the spark. The songbird is oblivious; fleeting warmth is all she felt. Staring into the brightening depths of the fire, she somehow misses and sees through the fire. Her vision blurs. The world recedes. It's like looking up at the world from beneath a water's surface, wanting to know where the blue sky crashes against the landscape like the ocean, the sky crashes against itself and in itself, light on light and blue on blue.

This is a sign. It means: *your chicks are dead!*
They are all dead!

PART TWO

"Get out! Get out! Get out!" shout the songbirds. "We know! We know! We know!"

"You don't *know*," the cuckoo answers shortly. Her voice is firm, but casual. "What do you know?"

"We know! You, you, all you cuckoos! Get out of the woods! Get out!"

"All right," the cuckoo says. "Attack me! I'll fight back! Do I look frightened?"

The cuckoo ducks as a songbird dives at her head, then straightens up again, ruffling out her feathers.

"Go ahead! Hit me! You can hit me but you can't beat me!"

"Egg-eater! Chick-killer!" the songbirds shout, working themselves up. "You're not so brave when you kill our chicks!"

"I've only just arrived here today!"

"You've been here forever! Get out!"

"If I've been here forever, then I should stay forever," the cuckoo says flatly. "You can hit me, but I've … I've …" The thought falters.

"Get out!"

"… I can take it!"

"Get out!"

"Are you going to kill me now? Are you going to kill me?"

"You're the killer! You're the killer!"

Another bird darts at the cuckoo's head. She ducks, feels the concussion of the bird's air wave like a slap, and, despite her resolute posturing, she retreats a little down the branch.

"I will defend my life!" the cuckoo warns. Then they come at her. "I won't be driven off!"

The cuckoo is flashing round and round through space, the air around her sizzles with lancing songbirds who veer in swiftly to snap, peck, and swerve away. The cuckoo pivots and dances through the air to avoid them, describing a crazy path that nearly collides with the ground and the trees. The cuckoo sprints for the sun and the upper air with all her might. The dazzle blinds some of her pursuers, the stronger gusts up high knock the smaller, lighter songbirds aside, or force them to overwork themselves. The mob of songbirds is reduced to the three largest males, who snap at her legs and tail. One of them yanks at her tailfeathers, and with a slight pang she feels one of them go. The surprise agitates her, and she flaps her wings in a blur, driving high into an airwave that swoops her up and away from her pursuers, flinging her out over open country and the bare hillsides. She pushes on mechanically until fatigue becomes pain in her shoulders and the lightness in her head. Below, a hillside, a short tree, a branch, see it, take it.

It is a relief to slack her wings. Her narrow chest seems to have two icy egg-shaped cavities in it, smarting and raw as a fresh scrape. There's a little curl of hunger down below getting stronger, too.

Well, that was bad, but it wasn't the worst. While she has no vivid recollection of any more serious encounters, she is certain she's had them. Why else would she be so wary now? She came here a long time ago, but she was clever and kept moving between several of these small woods, whose separations seem to confound her host-enemies. She is never pursued very far, and has always been able to slink back in again, usually within one hour. If the birds are particularly riled up, she just tries a different stand of trees, that's all. The only problem with the open spaces is hawks.

The day is bright and warm. That's right, start to take in the scenery and ease up. The sun mantling her sore shoulders is like a massaging hand. Her mate is around here somewhere, and soon it will be time for fresh pranks. Waves crashing on the shore whip coiling funnels of air up over the land, where the grass, rocks, and branches slow and eventually still their progress. The funnels turn to fraying salt rags and dissolve over the ground, soak into the lichens on the stones. The cuckoo watches the brilliantly colored spray disintegrating over the waves down below, then wafting in over the beach in white shadows that darken the egg-like heaps of rounded stones. The air frisks over the alert cuckoo, who is waiting for something. She decides to flit down and inspect the bracken for caterpillars or other provender, and drops down to a lower branch, noticing as she does so that there is a hollow in the tree here – a nest?

An empty nest, filling the basin at the bottom of the hollow, completely hooded by the tree. The wind eddies in the open space, making the down remnants shiver. Nothing here now, but carefully the spot is marked in her memory. Birds return to old nests sometimes. And opportunists will take advantage of an old nest, why not? The hollow has a pitchy smell, like fresh sap. Not unpleasant. There is, too, a faint odor of musty feathers and dry leaves. A good place to get out of the cold, since the nights are none too warm. How long will it be, she wonders, before the air really is warm? When the air is warm, her body opens. It's like coming out of a tight spot. She loves to sit dreamily in the open air on a warm night, invisible in her browns and greys, hearing the night sounds and knowing the other residents of the woods have been hard at work gathering food all day. My young are safe, she would think, invisible, hidden in plain view – safe, and well fed. One day they may have to face mobs of songbirds, but today those mobs work for them.

The songbirds are troublesome, but they're not as bad as hawks, falcons, and especially the owls. Owls, hawks, birds of that kind, they kill when they dive at you. And the owls can see you, can hear you, when you are too sleepy to watch, and they make no sound. They see through your disguise, which is why a nice little untenanted hollow like this is just the thing.

The sun is reaching its zenith, standing still overhead, quieting all below. The slurred hiss of the surf is an indistinct washing sound, and all the silence, the trance, sexually arouses the cuckoo. There is nothing more exciting than when everything is hypnotized and space becomes endless and secret. It won't be long before the cuckoo melts, slips through air and grass and trees like an otter spiralling through a clear pool of calm water, sliding out of the intangible secrecy of the afternoon to lay in a dozen nests. Invisible, watching, almost breathless with excitement, getting away with it over and over again.

Soon her mate will come back from wherever he is. Every now and then, the day stops – his voice is calling, not far away now, not too much longer to wait now. Waiting for him is torture! But ... go look for him? That would mean surrendering her only power over him. No matter how fiercely she expects him, she waits. She chose him, but then again, what choice did she have? She first saw him during a thunderstorm, before the rain began. The sky was ablaze with livid seams interspersed with dark masses, huge, inaccessible cloud nests, full of sun eggs that fractured and spat out flashing bolts of white and gold with terrible smashes, bright bursts of the light of embryonic days hatching out too early and dying. Then up there were countless little particles, birds, leaves, whatever the wind swept up toward the nests. From the stability of her perching place she watched this sky, seeing everything until she saw him, and then seeing nothing but him, as if he were alone in a black void, himself bright and clear and flashing inside the visible diamond outline formed by his beak, tail, and wingtips. The perfect straightness of his outline calls to him, using her voice; it is effortless, so that she barely hears herself. Against the chance eruptions of light and darkness and the flapping cascades of sound, the two of them swoop together on changeable wind, following the wind but always keeping together, passing each other, rising and dropping, braiding zigzags, staring wildly at each other, yellow-eyed, impassive as fiends, slicing the spiralling air before them with beaks like drawn daggers, feeling each explosion rap and shiver through them but not flinching when the light flares. Finally she alighted, unable to stand it, nearly exhausted, and he kept on flying inside her, his body the only point of light in a pupil of limpid blackness, turned, dove, swept up, flapped, teetered, with irresistible strength and effortless attention, showing his prowess in mastering the ceaselessly restless air. He was always flying, during and in between his visits. Always seeing. Always flying. And yet, when he called, his voice came to her from the heart of a motionlessness so perfect it stopped like another day, swelled, pushed the day aside, and englobed her for a moment in a landscape with him at its center, the domain of the carry of his voice. She stayed right where she was whenever she heard that; he would have to shift that center to her by coming to her. Instead of following his call, she let it fall on and all around her, becoming entranced by the way the sound faded into a silence that was like the sound of dust flowing on top of more dust; then she would snap out of it and answer, letting him know where she was, which was where he would have to go if he wanted her.

It's the songbirds that ruin it. Even splitting the open fields in a headlong rush to get to the cover of the trees and avoid the hawks has the thrill of daring to recommend it, but to be brutally awakened out of the seducing trance by the raucous cachinnation of furious songbirds, hideous and violent – that is abominable, that is the worst. To be swimming effortlessly from nest to nest, following expertly the promptings of each new circumstance, improvising like a master, the pulsation and bliss of delivery and escape mingled in one instant, repeated over and over and wanting it never to end, and then to be forced to jump and start, veer and duck in ugly vaults, fury barking all around in lacerating voices, fly away thwarted, insides steaming and unquenched, that is intolerable!

However, there is one songbird in the forest that is *much worse* than the rest. She does not come hurtling down on a cuckoo's head. She is eerily different, and has only to appear to chill the insides like icy water. Frigid water that pools in the gut like an independent animal, radiating a sickening cold and rolling with gravity, weighing the body down. A horrible piebald pink and black patch mars the bright plumage of the head and neck on the right side, and worse, the eye on that side is gone, and the frowsy white hairs of a fungus infection sprout from the socket instead. Even the other songbirds steer clear of that one. That one has never badgered her, never joined in the tirade with the others, because that songbird is crazy. She is conducting crazy affairs of her own, mad ventures, dream travels. She turns up, that's what she does. Every now and then, she turns up somewhere, as if she were everywhere. It's never possible not to expect her, and yet, whenever she turns up, she is simply sitting in place. Even though she travels as though she were searching all over for something, whenever she turns up, she doesn't act like she is looking for anything; she only ever turns up sitting somewhere quietly. If it were quiet she wanted, there is no end of it here. So why look for it? Does she want to try out all the quiets? From time to time it seems she sings. Different corners of the wood and the field resound in turn with a startling song, whose singer is never seen even though the singing always goes on and on. Female songbirds don't sing, of course, but no bird sings that way. The cuckoo herself has heard that song more than once; there's no mistaking it, even though it is impossible to remember. She knows she has heard that song she doesn't remember, because she does remember the way it made her feel; that feeling was unique in her experience.

At first, she had had no idea that what she was hearing was singing at all. The sound was nothing like any of the other sounds she could hear at the time. What she noticed first was an intermittent impression, weakly tugging at her attention, which, to be candid, was not fastened to anything in particular just then. Her attention was just ballooning slackly in front of her. After a while, the choice springing up out of a frisson of impatience, she curtly made note of the sound the way she might suddenly scratch an itchy spot, that is, it was necessary to dispense a minute amount of attention in order to return the distraction to its proper place, alongside all the other things that weren't worth bothering about. Itching returns sometimes even after it's been scratched, and sometimes an itch is a sign – of lice, for example; there are times when scratching an itch discovers a hitherto unnoticed injury, and times when scratching too vigorously damages the skin. This sound, once noted, took root in her attention. Its purchase on her grew. Because of the persistence of the sound, how long whatever was producing it went on, and because of the the insistence of the sound, she couldn't ignore it. The sound was not going to be like any other sound, in timbre or in behavior. It was determined to be different. It was only with effort, and experimentally, but still without being fully aware of what she was doing, that she identified the sound as singing, and it was because she couldn't feel satisfied with that designation that she continued thinking about it, so now she was listening.

The singing was sort of morbid. As she listened, increasingly fascinated by her own inability to connect what she was hearing to anything else she'd ever heard, she experienced a succession of associations, which flashed before her mind more abstract than concrete. She didn't see a rotting log toppling apart and fledged with gills, a stagnant pool all pricked with tiny bugs, the corpse of a baby chick squashed into the roots of a tree, the black scar where the dry grass had burned, the browning splash of blood on a stone where a hawk had paused to devour a sparrow ... All the same, somehow all these things occurred to her, not vividly, but all the more distinctly as they were passing. That singing was primarily the passage from one of these things to the other. Birds sit and sing. The song emerges from a given location and travels, but this song travelled like a moving bird, and made the cuckoo sit still, in order to travel with it, even though she didn't want to, didn't care. Ignoring it would mean acknowledging there was something to ignore, giving it an importance it shouldn't have, but then deciding not to ignore it, or rather ignoring that decision, had the same result. It seemed that any thinking at all led her into the song, which wasn't worth bothering about, but which for that reason irritated her. Was that birdsong, and was it a songbird? There was plainly only a single voice singing, but somehow the quality of the voice, what made it the voice of some sort of bird, was behind what it was singing, and couldn't be isolated. The voice was too quick and the changes it made were too drastic and swift. Each new tone cancelled the memory of the one that preceded it. That song might be only one note repeated over and over, simpler even than the cuckoo's own two-note call. No one saw what sang that song, but who else would sing like that, if not her? When not listening to the singing, which she heard more than once, the cuckoo can imagine that songbird singing, her tufted, sightless eyesocket turned in the cuckoo's direction but seeing her all the same. How bizarre that was! It gave you the creeps! The prospect of that bald scar and the opportunistic growth makes her shudder with repugnance, perhaps because she feels forced by the sight to imagine being that songbird, living with only one eye, and with a hideous appearance. There are times when she deliberately conjures the mental image in order to make herself feel good, though, to the extent that she is gratefully aware of the intact plumage on her own face, of her own two good eyes, and the regularity of her own voice.

No, there was some ominous promise in that song. To sing as if the rot itself were singing, the pain in the splash of blood or whatever it was that ground logs to crumbs and shat all over the flowers until they were mashed brown face down and shapeless into the mush, as if the moon were singing in the sky, darting leprous tangles of sound in all directions like moonshine, making land and sea ghoulish despite the colorlessness of the wind which for some reason can't blow this weightless lunar snow off the grass or the sand or the greedy rocks that seem to cultivate the gleaming moonlight that showers them, really shameless, basking in it like huge bulls rolling in moon muck. How many times had she, half asleep, mistaken the chill glamor of the full moon for daylight, and nearly flung herself into space, thinking the day had already begun, exposing herself to the vigilance of the unheard owl …

And now the fucking thing sings too! That is just the end! The cuckoo resents this reminder of the fatal world. What she likes is the soothing ratiocination of the breezes and waves, the motherly fluttering of the feathered wood like a vast brooding hen, a whole flock of them with long wooden legs and toes that knead the earth. Among the chorus of singing birds, who toss their voices like different colors that criss-cross and partially intermelt, there are still better notes that no one sings, little pauses, like gaps in a huge ghostly nest of voices, into which a dextrous and quick-witted cuckoo can slip a bit of something, smuggle a clever parcel of something. Among all the notes and pauses, she hears everything she knows. What does she hear? Eggs being laid, nests being made, a fluttering search for food, her own heartbeat of course – very important! – the abrupt calls of scrub jays, the lazy grating crows, accelerating thud of grouse. The breathing. The long riding whisper of the trees. The crash of surf in the distance. The plunks and hiccups of the stream, mumbling over rocks. The regular call of dogs. The meshed calls of other songbirds. The calls of mourning doves. The calls of snipes. The calling of crickets. If one were born free, one would, so long as one remained free, form no conception of good and evil …

… pulsing, breathing, barking …

… The virtue of the free is seen to be as great when it declines dangers, as when it overcomes them …

… pulsing, breathing, barking, crickets, snipe …

… Timely retreat as courageous, for the free, as combat; courage or presence of mind are shown equally well, whether the election be to give battle or to retreat …

… pulsing, breathing, barking, crickets, snipe, grouse, quail, surf, stream …

… the one who is free, and who lives among the ignorant, strives to avoid receiving favors from them ...

*

The carrion crows have discovered something big and dead in the tall grass. The wise cuckoo takes advantage of their distraction. A wise cuckoo waits for precisely such opportunities. It is almost a maxim. Unfortunately, it will be just as true for the songbirds, who fear crows too. If previous experience is any precedent, the current preoccupation of the crows will only cause the songbirds to turn their vigilance in another direction, rather than relax it. On balance, however, they are not the enemies the crows are, that is, songbirds will not kill a cuckoo endowed with ordinary luck. The eager peering of a watchful songbird will dial itself around every nearby object, but the almost haughty surveillance of the predators, the hawks, gulls, crows, takes in the whole landscape as impassively as if their eyes were dead. Everything within the plunging sweep of their vision is illuminated by banal death flat and plain as daylight. Only a potential rival elicits any expression. The clash of those deadly gazes precedes raising of the wings and opening beaks. Even though death is as inexhaustible and abundant as the air, and despite the great number of birds and other creatures for whom the landscape is a sprawling campus of death to the horizon, there is still room for some jealous jostling, for put-downs, and for vainglory.

It's a good thing the gulls do so well for themselves by the sea, they're such vicious brutes. They are so alien to the landbirds. That snowy whiteness over so much of them makes no sense in the dun and grey world of the woods. They're enormous, they stink like dead fish, and their voices are from a nightmare. Even their chicks are dangerous. Hawks, by contrast, are delicate, spiritual hunters. Proud, without being arrogant. Hawks are selective. A gull will rave at anything. But gulls are so blatant, they are not so difficult to avoid;

nor are they especially discerning creatures. Frankly, they are easily tricked by disguise, a little guile. A hawk is not so easy to hoodwink, and there is a hawk in the vicinity who makes a speciality of cuckoos. She has seen him regaling himself with one, lying limp and torn under his horrible talons. The hawk tears off a morsel of flesh from the cuckoo's breast, having pulled the ribcage apart and scattered the skin, then stands erect on its long legs, gripping the rag of flesh in its beak as if to display it. It is the hawk's impassive, wordless way of letting everyone know they are already his for the taking, whenever he should be so disposed, and as it was with this one, so it will be with you.

Crows are full of guile and seem to be chuckling merrily to themselves when they spring their traps and take their prey. The hawk devours the cuckoo as if it were almost beneath his notice, but crows take depraved delight in snaring their victims, and dance a jig when they return to a carcass. A crow may hunt alone or with others; there's no telling what they will do. By the time the black funnel forms, it is too late to take warning. The gull charges in from the sea, the hawk is a speck in the blue above one moment and on your back the next like a lightning bolt, but the crow comes from nowhere. His camouflage is so perfect it is invisible. Nothing could stand out more distinctly, at once clear and enigmatic, than a crow, and yet even sitting in plain sight it seems to evade detection until it is ready to act. Without being inconspicuous, without having to remain silent or stand stock still, the crow goes unnoticed, magically convincing its prospective prey that it is a stone, all black and croaking, or a thick root poking out of the ground with its thinner end sheared off. A shadow that glints like seawater on a grey day, one of those innumerable nameless things that human beings leave behind them everywhere, with their impossibly bizarre contours and jumbled textures, smells never before smelled and almost always freakishly heavy and solid. Then the attack – it's a crow, after all. A witty attack.

"Why didn't I see?" someone cries.

"Too late," the crow pounces. "Too late!"

"Why didn't I?"

"Too late!"

The crow settles down to brood on its treachery, clucking like a mother hen. It won't be long before its relations show up for their share, and, as they eat, the freeloaders ingratiate themselves to the killer by trading stratagems and reminiscing deliberately about the last time, when the guest was the host and the host was a guest. Crows understand disappointment, even if they don't feel resignation. Where the eye of a gull or a hawk gapes as an expression of its rapacity, a crow's eye asks an evil question, like night time – *will you live?* It's best not to think too much about crows; it only makes it more likely she'll choke when she encounters one.

"A crow is nothing but a slow hawk," she tells herself. "Slow and ugly. And they stink."

Crows pore over remains, forensic analysis is in their practical, utilitarian, unpoetic minds. Well, it's a stupid cuckoo who falls for a crow's wiles; a cuckoo has to know how to watch carefully, too, and a crow might learn a thing or two, might even be surprised, to learn just how sharp a cuckoo watches. Could a crow slip in and out of a nest unnoticed, discard one egg and lay another, all in the time it takes a wave to break against the shore? The deception must be perfect, and go unsung as well.

*

All in a moment the landscape is half-and-half blue shadows and livid light, like an instant snow shower, but it's a pulsing dart in the sky, racing down toward the mountains. It isn't lightning, though, because the sky is clear and black, and there's no sound at all. Light without sound and a neat line cooling its phosphors in her eyes now and slipping and sliding as the cuckoo blinks, startled, wondering if this strange greenish firefly light is anything to worry about. Nothing like lightning. No, nothing at all like lightning, this light was casual, almost furtive, except for that one guttering pulse that was like an error in flight, easily made, easily corrected. The sky winked at her, it seems.

"Did you see that?" she asks the plover, who is just happening by.

The plover does not answer, but draws herself up short, apparently startled.

"The light over there, did you see it?" the cuckoo asks.

"Light? What light? It isn't fire is it?" the plover's voice is hard edged. She builds her nest on the ground and has nightmares about brush fires, about standing helplessly by as her eggs cook, as her chicks burn.

"It was in the sky. It wasn't a star. It flashed and moved, then went out."

"I suppose I might have seen a flash," the plover says. "You don't think it's fire? Is that smoke I smell?"

"I think you're smelling human fires. They always have fires, it seems. You know what I think?" the cuckoo says, as if something has just occurred to her.

"No, I don't know what you think," the plover replies.

As if thinking were a disreputable habit, or, really, more like something the cuckoo was either not entitled to do, or something which, if the cuckoo were to do it, would produce nothing worth noticing?

"I'm thinking the songbirds are trouble these days," she says. "I'm considering changing to ground-nesting birds."

"Just try it," the plover snaps, raising her head high on her neck and hooding her eyes contemptuously.

"How well do you know those big eggs of yours?" the cuckoo needles.

"Quite well," the plover bats back. "Perfectly well."

"You're sure about that," the cuckoo observes.

"I should think I know the difference between a long leg and a short one!" the plover says, with venom. "I think I should know a long neck from a ... Well, you haven't much of a neck, have you?"

"Sharper eyes than yours have been fooled before," the cuckoo says, as if she were sincerely imparting advice.

"I'm not worried," the plover says. "I defend my nest. I'll come up on a dog – I don't give *A Fuck*. I've driven off cats. And I keep the rats away too, which is not exactly a straightforward job. At the first sign of any funny business –"

The plover flutters; she opens her wings and lowers her head, seeming to spread against the ground as she sinks. Then, demonstration concluded, she resumes her upright posture.

"Very impressive."

"You're the one who should be careful."

"Driving cats away must be exhausting. Watching for rats – where does it end, all the watching? That on top of all the feeding, I can't imagine how you manage the tedium ..."

"I'm sure you can't, my dear, any more than I can imagine having nothing at all to do all day."

"Oh, it's easy – very easy for such a clever bird as yourself, I'm sure. Just imagine doing exactly as you please."

"Well, it pleases *me* to be a *good* mother," the plover answers, looking off toward her nest. "... Someone gets us all in the end anyway. And so?"

⁑

The thunder has come again, dropping down in sections from the mountains toward the sea, as if whole avenues of ancient trees were collapsing one by one. The sun has almost set, the humid air is equal parts warm and cold, redolent of woodsmoke, the aroma of damp earth, now and then of brine.

A burst of light and a clash. A noise that crumbles hollowly away under the clouds. The old oak split by lightning glows down to its roots. The tree droops to the ground like a poleaxed bull and burns blood red. The songbird, drawn to the spot by a crash that still is echoing back in the woods, flutters up to take up a position in a thorn bush a dozen feet away from the burning tree. With her one good eye, she watches the flames, and above all she listens intently to the fire, then accompanies it, singing –

"Bodies are made of parts. Some parts are hard, some soft, some wet, some fire. Some are further inside than others … Body parts are vulnerable to other bodies and when a body made of fire causes another body's fluids to press on the soft parts of the body, it changes that body's shape and leaves a burn mark … bodies can act on, move, burn, and displace other bodies."

The stricken oak looks like the gaping jaw of an alligator, fanged with pointed white teeth that bob and shiver, belching foul breath and hissing explosively. Even so, it is still and dead. Only the fire lives. No animal eats like that, continuously, without needing to pause for breath or swallowing. Nothing could be so ravenous as this.

The plover pivots in place, watching as a bright orange, wind-tossed flame, stark against the cobalt-silver sky, traverses the open space above the grass in a straight line. She glimpses the underside of a violently flapping wing just within the fire, luridly shining golden underneath.

The cuckoo snaps out of a shallow sleep when the songbird alights on the rim of the hollow, the burning wind-whipped twig in her beak makes a violently flickering chaos of light inside the tree. The flame has caught at some of the feathers on the songbird's head, and devours the white tuft of its fungal infection a thread at a time, with tiny, wildly mobile sparks. The songbird opens her beak. The burning stick falls into the warm dry bed of twigs and leaves the cuckoo is lying on. At once, long guttering tongues of smutty yellow flame rise around the cuckoo with a liquid outline and searing heat. The cuckoo launches herself directly into a flurry of buffeting wings. The songbird's beak gashes the cuckoo's face, barely missing her left eye. The cuckoo flounders and falls back into the burning nest in confusion. A wingbeat flattens the fire, which curls back around on her and catches a patch between her shoulders. The sudden pain is like an impaling thorn screwing into her, and she goes wild, barrelling through the songbird and out, dazzled, into the indigo, out into the indigo and falling all the way to the ground, writhing and croaking, calling out in a voice she doesn't recognize as her own.

The songbird is perched and watching. Smoke streams from her feathers and the firelight whips shadows around a solitary and unblinking black eye reflecting a tumultuous golden streak.

Visible as thrashes against the muddy ground and lacerations of beautiful gold, vaguely lit by the smoke-muddled vision of the firelight from the nest as it twists a sturdy volute of fire up through the opening, scouring the edges of the hollow, the cuckoo is a silhouette against its own burning body, full round encircled in the black eye of the watching songbird, who remains where she is, despite the sparks that churn all around her, until the cuckoo lies still, dark in her own smoke.

*

Later, having wedged her burned body in among the roots of a solitary tree, the cuckoo is able to remain upright without effort and look out over the landscape.

"I still have my eyes," she thinks. "That's something. I could have lost them. One, or both of them. I would be blind now!"

The cuckoo watches the day develop. Thermals are forming as usual above the larger flat stones and bare spots; the soaring birds are lazily scaling thermals. Those columns of woven air will reach up above the level of the hills, then spread out in a cooling layer that will eventually settle down again, but as they rise, the sun hits those pillars of air and makes them fray and boil apart up higher. The canopy of cooler air rises all the time, spreading like a mushroom cap overhead. The long, nearly invisible legs of these colossal mushrooms stand all over the landscape, and the soaring birds use them – still climbing on legs after all, ha ha! They rise and then glide away when they get up enough, but only so as to come streaking down on their prey. A hawk goes veering by with something flopping in its talons, a mass of fur the cuckoo can't identify. Perhaps it was the burrowing creature that chased her from the mouth of its den earlier. She can't fly any more, her wings are too badly burned, so she had to crawl painfully over the ground, looking for a safe place to hide. It was only by fiat of that furry thing that she still lived; it had not struck at her, or even touched her, although it seemed angry enough at her intrusion. She suffered more in making her ungainly escape than from the creature's anger. A close call! But, as usual, she escapes. The pain, now that she isn't moving around, is everywhere, but not as sharp as before.

The hills form a gradual curve down onto the flatter space, rising up like waves, but not crashing down for some reason. The hills – and mountains, for that matter! – just rise and stop, keeping themselves up somehow. How how how? The water can't manage it.

Which is saying a lot; the water is so powerful she can't stand to go near it. Just the spray alone is so tingling and violent. So how strong does that make the silent mountains? It's an abstract power, unlike the manifest power of the hurtling wave. Which breathes up the cloud spray, which drives against the mountains like a second shore, travelling along the tops of the mushroom canopy, standing on its thermal legs, girdled by the lazy soaring birds. The soaring birds toboggan along the undulating tops of that canopy, in and out of the mist. The water birds bob on the surface of the water and sometimes dive under, with a little preparatory backward lunge, since water is pierced less easily than air, or so it seems. Not being a high flier herself, it's hard to know what the air is like up there.

Will she ever fly again? Her wings are burned naked as a chick's. Perhaps they will fledge again, the way they did when she was in the nest herself. It was a songbird who raised her. She remembers vividly the sensation of her foster-mother's beak being thrust into her throat. Too bad those days are over! She's famished! It was just dumb luck that led a blundering little bug to clamber up this root next to her; too late he saw her. She got the little fucker. It wasn't enough, but it was something. Her whole body exploded in pain the moment she had him, but that pain died down again in time.

She had been so jealous as a chick; she had to have foster-mother all to herself. There was no concept of "foster" at the time, only mother. It wasn't until she grew up that the cuckoo put all the pieces together. That was a shock! All that time thinking she was some kind of freak songbird, and then her instincts began and she understood it all. What a shock! But it was a relief, too. It meant that her indifference to male songbirds had been right all along; and all her fretting, her worries about being abnormal, had been nothing but silliness. She had known love, after all. And laid eggs. That was work done. It wasn't enough, but it wasn't nothing. She hadn't wasted her time.

Will she see her mate? Would he recognize her now? Will she ever see him again? Who knows? What's the use in wondering – she can tell him who she is, if she can manage to get her voice working again. Just now, while breathing is all right, any attempt to vocalize with her parched mouth and throat is uncomfortable, as though she had to break through a crust with her breath in order to make a sound. And opening her lungs, expanding her chest, beyond a certain point, is painful. Actually, acutely painful. So the voice will take time, but it probably will come back. If it would only rain a little, or if some dew would appear from wherever it comes from, she could test her voice. In the meantime, it would be good to sleep, but there's a faint but irrepressible excitement inside her still. Something happened to her. She was horribly burned. She will never be the same now – but how will she be? How different? Very different? Is it possible she might make a complete recovery, and be flitting lightly through the air once more, perhaps even in a few days? It doesn't seem that way. Perhaps not.

A songbird is singing, prettily, poor thing! Little do you know your chicks aren't yours. Had she laid any of her eggs in that wood this year? She must have, but she can't remember. Was it this year or the last? Was what? Was it this year or the last that she ignored the woods altogether, and laid all her eggs in those smaller copses in the groins of the hills? The songbirds were fewer there; in the woods there are a bit too many, the mobs over there are pretty scary. But then there was that hawk. A hawk likes to hunt around the smaller copses. It must have been away one year, which made it possible for her to nest her eggs there. Now the hawk is back, or at least a hawk. At least? She can't be sure it's the same hawk, other birds are so much alike. In all the woods, the only songbird she knows as distinct from any other is that burned one. She wonders where she saw the burned one last, but can't remember. What does it matter? It seems it should. Something important, involving that burned songbird. Ah. Yes. The fire.

Mist is thickening out there over the water, despite it being broad day out. The wind is cold just now, blowing on her and causing movement within her injuries, a new blossoming of pain across her front, but it is the kind of wind that changes direction. The cuckoo breathes open-mouthed, shivering. She did not get far from the tree, which is probably not burning any more. She still stinks of smoke, but the air is free of it. It occurs to her that her mate will swing by. He never has, but then that doesn't really matter; what he has done in the past and what he will do in the future don't seem to have much in common, not as far as he is concerned.

Out over the grass, clouds roll from position to position in the sky, seeming to knock against each other, and to send each other coasting into a different place. They walk in the meadow on thermal legs, with huge boulder feet. Birds shuttle up and down and side to side, weaving an intangible cobweb of faintly visible wakes. These straight wakes become scribbles without losing any order, it's surprising. "It is not in the nature of reason to regard things as contingent, but as necessary," she can hear them say, and then something more that she can't make out. The song is very far away. It doesn't say those words, but it does have that idea to it. The singing, the scribbled wakes, the thermals, and the clouds. Her mate is coming with some food in his beak for her. He'll perch on the root just by her head, and she will widen her mouth, and receive it from him like that. As she recovers, he'll have to make fewer and fewer visits. But he'll stay with her, just to keep her company. He never seemed to be the sort who would do something like that, but nothing prevents him from doing it. Perhaps he will come soon. The day seems to be darkening strangely, even though the sun is still fairly high. The sun is no less bright, but the sky around it doesn't hold its light. The daylight drains from the sky, curious! And the azure dims something like the nameless color of a dark reflecting puddle. Steadily dimmer and dimmer, a transparent kind of black clarity that she doesn't really see, which is more the bizarre absence of the sight of this one part of the world. The sun hangs in a thing she can't see, an even shadow. The songbird is singing in it; singing is foolish and difficult anyway. A few simple remarks, a head's up. The rest is silliness. Harmless.

That dark sky. Is it going to rain? There's too much sun for the rain. Then why so dark? There's sun, no night. It's too early for night. Isn't it?

If night falls, he won't come. It's a given, that, because of owls. Silent killers. But she's tucked away, the roots she lies among will keep her from being seen.

She's been lying in this spot for an incalculable time and has not been molested. It's a good spot for her. She's hidden, but her mate will find her anyway. He will know to look for her when he sees the nest is burned out. She won't be able to call him, not with her throat so dry, but she will want him so much that he will come to her and feed her.

The ocean seems to be boiling. It is flooding upright. That is, the mist is lifting from the waves in a dense, steady exhalation, making the sea so misty she can only barely make out the curling edges and subsidences of the larger waves, nothing but lines and angles. The gulls, the wind. A dog barks. The songbird stops singing. Has it been singing?

The wind-driven waves drive the wind onto the land, driving the leaves and anything loose into the grass, rolling over and over. Leaves flap in the wind. Grass flaps in the wind.

Windy here, mist ascending straight there. Isn't it an inconsistency? The cuckoo wonders – What is this frightful shape that is coming?

The mist thickens and the shape becomes more distinct.

Is it coming? Or standing up, like mountains in the ocean? Or has she somehow gotten turned around, or is she – has she been facing the mountains all along? So then it's the hills that are moving in place, spinning like wallowing pigs. Black points the erect ears of the horses and cows cut the gold into moted beams, lay them across the pigs to the sea where the beam ends beat back the mist and drive it down. That isn't happening, though. Instead, the mist hardens in the sunlight escaping into it and that angled horror is more obvious all the time, colossal as a mountain, with a mountain's high points, but down below the peaks the mist still occasionally parts to show the ocean. The dark points bob in space. Those clearings in the mist seem to fly out from her eyes like holes, plunge forward into the mist bringing the sight of a curling bit of froth or a stone or scrap of kelp into distincter focus for a moment before leaning out again and swinging off to the side.

It is a monster owl the size of the woods, with as many elbows in its wings as the woods has treetops, mute, soaring down to grab the landscape in its talons and fly off with it. The two ear tufts very slowly spread apart as the owl beats to the shore, as if it were swimming through the mist. The wind cuts cold, and whatever isn't pinned down is somersaulting past her. There goes a bundle of bright feathers, tossed up and landing with an almost animated patness, only to flip up and travel further along with the next gust, the sticklike legs are up and stiff and dry as sun-brown pine needles. A songbird's body, so light it barely rests on the ground; it catches on a little knot of grass, the wind scoops it up and sends it on its way again, and it vanishes in tall grass, strangely wind-tossed grass in stationary mist that stands everywhere now. Very misty today.

It is a fine, even whiteness, more color than light for a change. A nice change; the cuckoo is soothed.

APPENDIX: ETHICS (for birds) Part One

Concerning Hatching

<u>Definitions</u>

1. What hatches creates an echo, beginning before singing, before there is a voice, and it is that which resonates already within the living egg.
2. Any thing that is gestating is considered to be a living egg, that is, within a shell. To be gestating is preparation for singing, for any calling entity. For example, a body is considered to be finite because we can always conceive of its hatching out into a new and still developing singer. So, too, a thought hatches another thought. But the singing body is thinking, and the song of thought starts out as a body.
3. Scintillation is that which broods and hatches itself; its gestation requires another thing from which it has receded.
4. Thinking about scintillation is accompanied by phrasings.
5. Mood is the kind of scintillation, that is, the particular way in which something is hatching into something else.
6. Teemingness is the shadow, moonlight, or night remembrance of day, that is, the image of scintillation, consisting of any hatching which is free to create echoes, to resonate without ending.
7. A thing that echoes in all directions, and is teeming, is free. A thing is considered to be unhatched or unfledged if it exists and acts in a faltering way.
8. Neverendingness is expressed in the echo.

Axioms

1. All things hatch into the outside.
2. What cannot be hatched itself must be brooded.
3. Hatching follows from brooding, and the chick follows from the egg, and the egg follows from the nest; and all things live this way.
4. The knowledge of a brooding depends exclusively on the knowledge of a hatching.
5. Only things which have nothing in common with each other can recede through each other; the receding of the song does not involve the receding of the trees, the sounds heard through the shell have nothing in common with the egg.
6. A true conception must hatch with any and all broodings.
7. If an egg can be conceived as not hatching, its essence involves echoing, and is an echo, rather than a song.

Propositions

1. Scintillation is by nature simultaneous with all hatchings.
2. Scintillation has nothing else in common with itself.
3. Only the layer can cause the egg.
4. Two or more distinct chicks are distinguished from one another by their calls.
5. Scintillation can only exist in the landscape.
6. Scintillation can only be caused by what is not scintillation.
7. The echo belongs to the nature of scintillation.
8. Scintillation is free.
9. The more echo or being a thing has through the shell, the more it recedes.

10. Each hatching of scintillation must be conceived through its receding.

11. The echo of scintillation consisting of free phrasings, each of which expresses neverending and free receding, and is also free.

12. No phrasing of scintillation itself can be truly hatched, from which it would follow that scintillation consists only in more egg laying.

13. Free scintillation is neverending recedingness of the mother's voice.

14. There can be, or be conceived, only other scintillations.

15. Whatever is, recedes, and nothing can be layed or hatched without receding.

16. From the freedom in the air there must follow free travels in free ways (that is, everything that can be produced by a mother's voice, freely echoing).

17. Scintillation acts solely against the confines of its egg, and hatches only to lay.

18. Resonation of the mother's voice through the shell is the transitive cause of all things.

19. Scintillation is neverending, that is, all of the phrasings of teemingness are neverendingly hatching.

20. The echo of teemingness and the hatchings of the newborns are one and the same.

21. All eggs that hatch from the absolute receding of teemingness have no mother.

22. Whatever follows from some phrasing of a mother, exists freely, as an echo.

23. Every mother's song which exists freely must have freely followed either from the absolute nature of some phrasing of a song or from some phrasing modified by a free modification.

24. The essence of eggs layed by the singing mother requires that they be beneath her body.

25. The echo through the shell is the efficient cause not only of the hatching of things but also of their avian phantomishness.

26. What acts as expected is expected by teemingness, and an egg that teemingness expects is also itself expecting a hatching to come.

27. A thing which has been expected by teemingness to act in a particular way remains surprising.

28. Every individual thing must be under the body of its mother.

29. Everything is surprising, like the precise appearance of the newborn, but all things are from the free teeming of scintillation, surprising to recede, surprising to approach. The father's song is always surprising.

30. The finite voice in action or the free voice in act must comprehend the phrasings of teemingness and the recedings of teemingness, as well as everything else.

31. The voice in singing or calling must be related to the song singing, not to the song sung.

32. Song cannot be called a free cause, but only a surprising effect. The father is always willful.

33. Things could only have been hatched by teemingness in any other way or in any other order than is the case.

34. Songs are haunted by their very power.

35. Whatever we conceive to be within the song's power, the song will accomplish.

36. Nothing exists from whose receding a brooding does not follow.

APPENDIX: ETHICS (for birds) Part Two

Of the Nature and Origin of Song

<u>Definitions</u>

1. A body is a feathering thing whose outcryings recede in the teemingness.
2. What is crying out, when hatched, is what it had been crying out to be when unhatched, and when hatched is no longer an avian phantom. Something that is will make some outcry.
3. An idea is the echo of scintillation which takes place in the outcry; the fledgling is learning to sing.
4. A neverendingly resonant outcrying is one which, without relation to the mother, must always be correct, and cannot be misunderstood or misheard.
5. Livingness is the participation of a thing in neverendingness by way of resonant receding.
6. Neverendingly resonant and perfect mean the same thing.
7. An individual thing is that which hatches from scintillation and outcries in a receding way. It is in coordinated, simultaneous action by the flock at once that the teemingness of individuals can be seen.

<u>Axioms</u>

1. The horizon exists independently of the outcry that it attracts.
2. Outcriers are learning to sing.
3. Moods of singing, such as love, the desire to excrete, or whatever emotions are designated by name, do not occur unless there is in the same individual the idea of the

recession of the thing loved, excreted, etc. But the idea can be without any other mood of singing.

4. There are many way to fly to the horizon.
5. The ouctrier does not feel or perceive any individual things except what hatches from scintillation and recedes toward the horizon.

<u>Propositions</u>

1. Song is an attribute of teemingness, or teemingness is a singing.
2. Land and sea are a phrasing of teemingness, or teemingness is land and sea.
3. In teemingness there is necessarily not only the song of land and sea, but also of all things which are always found on the land or in the sea.
4. The song of teemingness, from which an infinite number of things proceeds, is still just one song.
5. All songs are caused by teemingness, only insofar as teemingness is a singing thing, not insofar as it is sung.
6. The moods of any given phrasing are caused by teemingness sung through the moods of an outcrier's growing body.
7. The order and connection of phrasings is the same as the order and connection of things.
8. All the songs that do not exist must be heard in the infinite song of teemingness, in the same way as the types of singers or moods are brooded in the hatchings of teemingness.
9. The song of a thing is caused by teemingness because the song is affected by another song of a thing, and so on without end.
10. The hardness of teemingness does not extend to the singer – so, scintillation does not make up the actual meat and

feathers of the singer.

11. The first element is the song of somebody.

12. Whatsoever comes to pass in the song must affect the singer's voice, or there will necessarily be a song of that event in the singer's unvoiced voice. That is, if the event occupying the singer is a body, nothing can take place in that body without becoming part of the song.

13. The burden of the song is the body, that is, a certain mood of the land or sea which actually exists, and that is all.

Axiom I: All bodies are either moving or not moving.

Axiom II: Moving bodies move at different speeds.

> Lemma I: Bodies are told apart by their speeds, and by whether or not they move, and not in any other way.
>
> Lemma II: This is true of all bodies.
>
> Lemma III: Bodies are moved by each other, so all motion is one singing.

Postulates:

> First, the body is made of different parts.
>
> Second, some parts are hard, some soft, some wet, some firm.
>
> Third, the body's parts are vulnerable to other bodies.
>
> Fourth, the body depends on other bodies to continue in that form.
>
> Fifth, when some body compels a body's fluids to press on the softer parts of the body, it changes that body's shape and leaves a mark.
>
> Sixth, the body can act on, move, and rearrange other bodies.

14. The outcrier is capable of perceiving a great number of

things, in proportion as its body is capable of receiving a great number of impressions.

15. The song is not simple, but compounded of a great number of phrasings.

16. The song of every mood must involve the nature of the outcrier and also the nature of other bodies.

17. If the outcrier is affected in a manner which involves the nature of any external body, the outcrier will regard the said external body as actually existing until the outcrier be affected in such a way as to lose the external body.

18. If the outcrier has once been affected by two or more bodies at the same time, when the singer afterwards sings any of them, it will remember the others also, and learn.

19. The singer has no knowledge of the body, and does not know it to exist, save through the modifications whereby the crying out affects the growing body. For example, the calling that causes feeding.

20. The song of the singer is also in scintillation, just as the song is in the singer's body.

21. Singing is united to the song in the same way as the singing is united to the body.

22. The outcrier perceives not only being fed, but the calling to be fed.

23. The outcrier does not know itself the way its mother knows it, except in so far as it learns to feed itself.

24. The outcrier does not have adequate knowledge of the parts composing the body.

25. The songs of being fed do not involve any really adequate knowledge of the external body.

26. The outcrier does not have any knowledge of other bodies, except insofar as it first learns that its mother does not intend to continue to feed it indefinitely.

27. The idea of being fed does not involve an adequate knowledge of the body itself.

28. The idea of being fed is not clear and distinct, but confused.

29. The idea of being fed does not involve an adequate knowledge of the mother.

30. We can only have a very inadequate knowledge of the duration of our body.

31. We can only have a very inadequate knowledge of the duration of our mothers continuing to feed us.

32. The ideas of being fed, and of the mother's unwillingness to continue doing it, insofar as they refer to scintillation, are true.

33. There is nothing positive in the ideas of being fed, or of the mother, which causes them to be called false.

34. The idea of being fed, and of the mother, which in us is absolute or adequate and perfect, are true.

35. Falsity consists in the privation of food which arises as a result of inadequate, fragmentary, or confused ideas.

36. Being fed insufficiently, or being fed poorly, follows as necessarily from events, as does being fed to satisfaction.

37. That hunger which is common to all (cf. Lemma II., above), and which affects the whole body as much as it affects the stomach, is not something apart from the body that feels it.

38. Hunger, which is common to all, and which is equally in a part and in the whole, cannot be conceived except adequately.

39. Hunger will be represented by an adequate idea in the outcrier.

40. Whatsoever ideas in the mind follow from hunger are also themselves adequate.

41. Knowledge of the first kind is the only source of falsity,

hunger is necessarily true.

42. Hunger, not knowledge of the first kind, teaches us to distinguish the true from the false.

43. The outcrier who is hungry simultaneously knows that he has a true idea, and cannot doubt of the truth of the hungriness perceived.

44. It is not in the nature of reason to regard things as contingent, but as necessary.

45. Hunger necessarily involves the neverending echo of scintillation.

46. The knowledge of the neverending echo of scintillation which hunger involves is adequate and perfect.

47. The outcrier has an adequate knowledge of the neverending echo of scintillation.

48. The hungry outcrier has no absolute or free will; but is determined to wish by hunger, which has also been determined by another hunger, and this last by another hunger, and so on to infinity.

49. There is in the hungry outcrier no volition or affirmation and negation, save that which a hunger involves.

APPENDIX: ETHICS (for birds) Part Three

On the Origin and Nature of Mating

Definitions

1. Where mating follows singing, there is adequate cause. Where mating occurs, but does not follow singing, this is an inadequate or partial cause, since such a succession of events cannot be understood.
2. One is active when one sings or responds to singing, and hence is the adequate cause of mating. One is passive insofar as one does not sing, or does not respond to singing. Where mating occurs passively, it takes place inadequately, which is to say under conditions of only partial causality. Inadequate mating arises owing to some other event.
3. The desire to mate, or to sing, entails a modification of the body, as the body grows capable of mating and of singing. If the body is diminished, it is less able to mate or to sing. Also the song itself will be correspondingly modified.

Postulates:

1. The adult body can be affected in many ways, only some of which will affect its ability to mate.
2. The body can undergo many changes, and, nevertheless, retain the impressions or traces of objects and of songs.

Propositions:

1. The adult body seeks out mates both actively, by singing, and passively, by listening.
2. The body cannot compel a song to come to it by listening, and the singer cannot compel a body to come to it where

its song goes unheard.

3. Mating is incomplete without singing, even when it results in brooding.

4. No brood can be destroyed, except by a cause external to itself.

5. Things are naturally dangerous which are capable of harming broods.

6. All living things strive to continue to live.

7. This striving is singing.

8. The song has no beginning or end, because the striving has no beginning or end.

9. Those who hear the song do not listen for beginnings or endings in the song, but only in their own inclination to listen.

10. Every song emerges from a singing body.

11. Whatever strengthens the body, fortifies the song. Whatever sustains the listener to listen for the singing, also fortifies the song.

12. The singer therefore seeks out what strengthens the singing body, while the listener seeks out what sustains the listening body.

13. The singer and the listener both correspondingly also avoid whatever weakens the body, and so diminishes the singing.

14. When one hears the song of love, love appears in the hearer. When love appears in the singer, it appears in the singing.

15. Anything can, accidentally, cause pleasure, pain, or desire.

16. The first song of love one hears will echo without ending. That song will always be receding within later songs.

17. If the song of love does not attract a mate, or if the song is heard, but the singer undesirable, then that song will also continue to echo without ending.

18. The echo of the song continues to have phantomish power.

19. The one whose mate dies will suffer. The one whose mate still lives will rejoice.

20. The prey rejoices when a predator dies.

21. When the mate rejoices, one rejoices also. When the mate suffers, one also suffers.

22. One rejoices to see what rejoices the mate. One suffers to see what causes the mate to suffer.

23. The prey rejoices to see what kills the predator. The prey suffers to see the predator consume any prey.

24. The prey suffers to see those who rejoice to see the predator, and rejoices in seeing those who fear the predator.

25. All who live seek out rejoicing and avoid suffering.

26. All prey rejoice at the sight of what will kill the predator, and recoil from the sight of what strengthens it.

27. One feels what the song feels.

Corollary I.— If the sound of the song is seductive, we are seduced. If it is not seductive, we are not seduced, and may be repelled.

Corollary II.— If the song seduces us, we cannot hate the singer.

Corollary III.— If the song seduces us, we seek to attend further on the singer.

28. The singer therefore sings as seductively as possible, and does not put into the song those feelings which cause hatred.

29. The singer will also try to seduce as many as possible, and to be seductive at all times.

30. If the singer is seducing listeners, then the singer will rejoice. The seductive singer rejoices in being seductive. The repellent singer suffers in being repellent, and does not

simply cause suffering to others.

31. When the listener sees that the song seduces others as well, the listener's seduction will thereby be deepened. When the listener sees that the song fails to seduce others as well, the listener will begin to second-guess their ears.

32. Since only one mate may be had by each, one who seeks to mate with a certain other will try to drive off any rival.

33. When the singer is heard and fully understood, it can be assured that the singer and the listener have an understanding.

34. The more fierce the desire for the mate, the more the desired mate may play hard to get.

35. The singer who is passed over will hate the listener and envy his rival.

36. The singer who finds a mate rejoices in the song.

Corollary.—A singer who is passed over will never sing that song again without suffering.

37. The roaring fire of mating grows with rejoicing and is quenched by suffering. Reason is a roaring fire.

38. The roaring fire of mating causes the one who is not chosen the greater suffering, if the one who is not chosen has sung with the greater desire.

39. The one who suffers will want to return harm without risk. The one who rejoices in another will want to cause that one to rejoice.

40. The one who sings and is passed over will be mollified by the sight of others who have been passed over by the same listener.

41. A poor singer who understands its song is poor and is preferred anyway will be grateful.

Corollary.— The one who is preferred by one he does not want will both hate and love that one.

42. The singer who is heard, but ignored, suffers.
43. The rivalry of singers is not felt until the selection is made.
44. The rivalry of the preferred singer disappears.
45. The rivalry of the one who is passed over will be fiercer.
46. The singer who is preferred over rivals regards them and rejoices, and sees all others as rivals over whom one rejoices. The one who is passed over regards rivals and suffers, and sees all others as preferred ones. If a rival with some noteworthy plumage is preferred, the one who is passed over will feel pain whenever seeing any other also having plumage of that kind.
47. While the prey rejoices in the suffering of a predator, this rejoicing is not unmixed with pain.
48. The terror of one notable predator is not lessened as one sees other predators of that species.
49. The fear of the predator is necessary for life; while precious, it is not the same as the affinity for the mate, which is particular for the preferred.
50. Anything whatever can be, accidentally, a cause of hope or fear.
51. The same song will not always be heard to be the same by several listeners, and the same song that left us indifferent at dawn may move us as the sun is going down.
52. A thing in a flock does not hold the attention for as long as a thing on its own. It is the flock one sees.
53. To hear oneself sing well, or to be sung well to by another, causes rejoicing. To hear the song grow and become better is to rejoice, whether one sings it or only receives it.

54. The singer wants only to sing better.
55. The poor singer suffers for being poor at singing.

Corollary.—The song of the songbird is not measured against the songs of quails.

56. Feeling is a roaring fire, with as many shapes and colors. Feeling arises as quickly and vanishes as quickly. Feeling is the sky.
57. The singer does not feel what the listener feels. This is what makes them what they are.
58. Not all rejoicing is a matter of hearing. There is the rejoicing of mating, which is not altogether like listening.
59. Mating is the best rejoicing.

APPENDIX: ETHICS (for birds) Part Four

Of Nesting

Definitions

1. Good nesting material is light, durable, and easily assembled.
2. Poor nesting material is whatever hinders the assembly of a nest.
3. Chance governs the availability, but not the discovery, of good nesting materials.
4. The creation or refurbishment of a nest is always possible, and this means that the ability to create or refurbish a nest is present.
5. Conflicting emotions arise after mating.
6. Emotion is an element of mating, but becomes an element of nesting insofar as nesting proceeds from mating.
7. Nesting is an expression of a desire for brooding.
8. Skill refers to the ability to find good nesting material, to avoid poor nesting material, and to construct from good nesting material a good nest.

Axiom:

There is no nest so well put together that the falling of the tree, the sundering of the lightning, the blaze of the fire, or the onslaught of the wind, may not ruin it. There is always something stronger that can destroy any given thing.

Propositions:

1. Poor nesting materials that have been mistaken for good

nesting materials will continue to appear to be good nesting materials even when they are clearly understood to be poor.

2. The nest builder who simply throws together nesting materials is a passive nest builder.

3. Life is a limited thing independent of any consideration of predators, injury, hunger, or disease. Even one who escapes all these remains exposed to greater powers, most notably that power which causes one to shrink and fail.

4. While the impulse to nest and to brood is without end, the nest builder and brooder in person is by nature not without end.

Corollary.—Hence it follows, that the impulse to nest and to brood do not fail, but only the one who may nest or brood, that this is nature, and that one cannot avoid growing older in the same motion that brings one into the frenzy of mating in the first place.

5. The nest is a small structure in a vast forest. The impulse to nest and to brood arises in the nest builders, the mated couple, but is also affected by external circumstances in which they find themselves, and which greatly overpower them.

6. As with singing and with mating, the nesting impulse can overcome all others.

7. So all impulses are not solitary, but sing in a chorus such that some drown out the others. The impulse to sing can destroy the impulse to nest, but the impulse to nest cannot be destroyed by a song any more than the nest itself can.

8. The nest builder knows how to build the nest only to the extent that the nest builder is aware of what they are doing.

9. The impulse to nest is stronger in the nesting spot, or in the presence of the incomplete nest, than it is far away.
10. Concern about the condition of the nest, the eggs, or the chicks, lessens only when the current condition of the chicks and the nest is known. This anxiety increases the moment one departs, and does not abate until one returns to the nest. However, this anxiety will grow steadily as the interval separating departure and return grows.

Corollary.—One never worries about nests one no longer uses. When the young are fledged and departing, the nest is all but forgotten.

11. Nest construction and brooding are more important than bathing, fully satisfying one's own hunger, or one's own need for rest.
12. The attachment to the unhatched egg is stronger than the attachment to the unhatched chick.

Corollary.—Though the chick somehow be inside the egg, until it is hatched, it is like a cloud on the horizon, and no more.

13. The attachment to the chick that may or may not hatch today is greater than the attachment to those chicks who have hatched, fledged, and gone away.
14. Fear arises when danger is noticed, but the power to affect us is in the danger, and not in the noticing.
15. The desire to mate is quenched by the desire to brood. The desire to use the mouth for singing or eating is checked by the desire to use the mouth to procure and carry nesting material.

16. The desire to brood is less than the desire to mate before mating, and greater than the desire to mate after mating. The desire to brood comes after the desire to mate.

17. The desire to flee predators is almost completely dormant when there are no predators near.

18. Desire arising from pleasure is stronger than desire arising from pain.

19. Feeding, singing, mating, nesting, brooding, are desired. Starvation, laryngitis, social ostracism, nestlessness, childlessness, are avoided.

20. The more one can feed, the better one can sing, the more often that one can mate, nest, and brood, so much the better for that one; that is the right kind of life. The more one goes hungry, the more poorly one sings, the more ignored one is at mating time, to that extent, life does not go well.

21. No one can have the desire to feed, to sing, to mate, to nest, to brood, and not desire to live, since that is living.

22. Any other good thing apart from these is unimaginable.

Corollary.—There is nothing to be gained by trying other things than these.

23. Without mating, singing, feeding, nesting, brooding, there is no life.

24. Where there is no life, nothing other than these things can be tried, because what does not live is not able to try anything.

25. One mates and broods for oneself, not for one's chicks.

26. Sitting on the nest, or hastening back to the nest with food, one conceives of all manner of things, but only insofar as these things will make nesting and brooding happen.

27. What one conceives as desireable or not, or what one sets oneself to get or to do, is determined in keeping with these fleeting reflections.

28. What is best is to be familiar with scintillation; those who are happiest, who live best, do so by being thoroughly familiar with scintillation.

29. The weather buffets just like the wingbeat of an eagle, the sickness weakens us just like the fatigue brought on by our own exertions, the predator eats us just as we eat our food. What causes us harm is therefore similar to us. The grass does nothing to hurt us and the trees do not make nests from feathers for themselves.

30. What harms us is what thrives through harming us, because it is feeding.

31. And so, what harms us acts for itself, and what helps us also acts for itself, but in a way that is not harmful.

32. In feeding, mating, singing, nesting, and brooding, it is not uncommon for there to be strife.

33. While what is good is good for all, there is not always enough of what is good, so that all may have what is good.

34. Where there is not enough of something good for all who desire it, there will be combat.

35. Combatting is good for the winner, and bad for the loser.

36. It is best when all are able to have all good things.

37. As one is familiar with scintillation, one sees that the having of good things by others is also good for oneself.

38. Anything that makes the getting or doing of good things easier is good.

39. Whatever makes the distances shorter, the days longer, the vision clearer, the food more abundant, the flock larger, is good. Whatever makes distances longer and days shorter, vision cloudier and food scarce, whatever reduces the size

of the flock is bad.

40. The larger your flock, the less likely the predator will get you.
41. Pleasure in itself is not bad, but pain in itself is bad.
42. Singing cannot be excessive; contrariwise, remaining silent at dawn is always bad.
43. Insofar as hunger causes one to do more, it is good.
44. Desire may be excessive.
45. Hatred can never be good.

Corollary I.—Hatred is the persistence of the terror of the predator, the combative impulse, the rejection of the impostor, where these things no longer are.

Corollary II.—Whatever such feelings cause one to do is a hindrance to the getting or doing of good things, and so is bad.

46. Combatting too hard can maim or kill. This makes the flock smaller. See 40.
47. Issuing warnings when danger is near helps to keep the flock larger.
48. If one finds food and does not inform the others, this is because the food is eaten, or to be taken to the young. Feeding the young will enlarge the flock.
49. The young are young because they cannot fly, and so cannot feed themselves.
50. The young cease to be young when they become able to fly, and so find their own food.
51. Brooding does not continue indefinitely, but has an end.
52. Brooding does not end when the young become large, and begin to fledge.
53. Brooding can end only when the fledged young are able to fly, and so find their own food.

54. Brooding ends only when the parent causes the fledged young to abandon the nest.

55. The desire to brood therefore must become the desire to bring brooding to an end.

56. The desires of the parents are nested in their young as the young are nested by the parents.

57. The desires of the parents become the desires of the young, but without ceasing to be active in the parents as well, just as one fire may create another without itself diminishing.

58. When the parents no longer desire, they may yet act out of memory.

59. The pain that comes when the young leave prompts the return of the desire for brooding.

60. The desire for brooding cannot be excessive, because the sorrow that comes when the young leave is boundless.

61. Consideration of what suffering might come to the young after they leave will affect the parents as strongly as the recollection of the current or past sufferings of their young.

62. Fear for the young exacerbates the memory of their departing, but cannot itself prompt the desire for brooding.

63. The destiny of the young is unknowable after they leave.

Corollary.—Hence, the departure of the young is a final parting, in which death and life look alike.

65. The suffering of the parents after the departure of the young is still to be preferred over the misery of those who have never brooded any young at all.

Corollary.—Therefore, the suffering of the parents after the young have departed is good, although painful. The suffering of the one who has never mated is far worse, although that one never knows the suffering of the parent whose young has departed.

66. The departed young restore the flock, and may expand it, and this benefits all. The benefit is greater than the suffering of the parents after the young have gone.
67. While parting is like death, remember that it is not.
68. The departure of the young endows both the parents and the flock with life, rather than diminishing it.
69. Those who never mate do not suffer the departure of the young, but have failed to endow the flock, and consequently themselves, with more life.

Corollary.—So the happier ones will console themselves when the young have departed.

70. The happier ones will continue to sing.
71. The young show their gratitude to their parents by ceasing to rely on them.
72. The departure of the young is what holds the flock together.

73. The young always depart, and the ones who are alone will be more alone when they leave. Only those who live in a flock will not be alone after the young have gone.

APPENDIX: ETHICS (for birds) Part Five

Of Nameless Later Happenings

Axioms:

1. When the predator stalks the prey, either the prey will escape, or it will not escape. When sickness or injury occur, the sufferer either recovers, or does not recover.
2. The prey that escapes the predator is no less susceptible to being stalked again. The sick or injured one who recovers is no less susceptible to becoming sick or injured again.

Propositions:

1. The terrors of the forest, of the open meadow, of the upper sky, of the hillside, of any landscape, are as terrible in thought and song as they are for the one who is there.
2. The terrors of the landscape can only be considered by one who is not in danger. To depart the landscape of terror, and to find refuge, is necessary if one is to think on terrors without the attendant sensations of terror.
3. To think on the terror of the landscape is to become capable of naming the nameless happening.

Corollary—The ability to name that which affects us, but which is nameless, is a new song the singer sings in a different landscape.

4. There is no modification of the body, whereof we cannot form some clear and distinct conception.

Corollary.—Terror as a modification of the body can therefore be understood, but not while it is in effect. Terror in body is now. The song of terror is a memory.

5. Terror is the most powerful of all feelings, because it is the body's feeling for itself; terror echoes with increasing noise in the flesh and bone. It is the warning called by blood to itself.

6. The thought of terror is therefore the most powerful thought; only the greatest thought could encompass it, as the whole of the mind must be taken up with it just as the whole of the body is. Terror does not afflict the body only in one or another of its parts.

7. The thought of terror is itself terror, because it is not terror of a predator, an injury, a sickness, or the violence of the weather, but must be what is the same in all these things.

8. To be afflicted with more than one cause of terror does however compound terror.

9. The thought of terror is not a compound of all possible terrors, but rather the voice of all possible terrors.

10. It is necessary to be safe in order to realize terror.

11. Terror is the greatest thought because it can be applied to the greatest number of possible threats.

12. It is in the conceiving of threats that caution is realized.

13. The song of terror, when sung with the sounds of caution, becomes the song of warning, and hence, the song of safety.

14. The singer can sing the song of safety so that it recedes to the horizon of all of scintillation.

15. It is the lover of safety who thinks of terror, so as best to sing the song of safety.

16. Nothing is more important than loving safety, and

therefore, without fear, to think of terror.

17. Scintillation is not a predator.

Corollary.—The predator acts upon its instincts which are particular to it, while scintillation is greater. The predator is a part of scintillation, but scintillation does not prey on the living.

18. No one can hate scintillation.
19. Scintillation is not a mate, or a member of the flock.
20. Love towards scintillation is needed if terror is to be thought without fear, and so it is good; the more in the flock who love scintillation, think terror, and sing safety, the safer the flock.
21. The singer can sing only as long as the body lives.
22. Although the predator may catch the prey, the injury or sickness may induce a *nameless effect*, or it may be that the *nameless effect* occurs for reasons that are unclear, the flock continues to live and scintillation continues to reveal more living bodies.
23. While a *nameless effect* may cause a body to stop singing, there will always be bodies, and there will always be singing.
24. Scintillation is understood moment by moment.
25. The one who thinks the thought of terror without feeling afraid is thinking the thought of scintillation.
26. There is no relief from the terror but the thought of scintillation.
27. The song of scintillation is an escape from the terror by way of the terror.
28. The relief the song of scintillation brings increases with the singer's emphasis.
29. The thought of scintillation is like the horizon; it can never

be approached, but always remains at a constant distance away, and returns the echoes that recede toward it.

30. The singer is a part of scintillation even after the last brooding.
31. The song of scintillation is the song of the singer.
32. Even after the *nameless event*, the scintillation continues.
33. As having young preserves the flock, so singing scintillation extends the existence of the singer, since the singer is in the song as well.
34. While the body weakens, the song does not.
35. Scintillation loves itself.
36. Singing is our way of expressing that love, which can only come into being through the doings of the living.

Corollary.—The cold, the hungry, the sick, the exhausted, should not hate life, even if they are no longer able to sing.

37. Hearkening to the song is better than nothing.
38. Don't be afraid; the *nameless event* is death.
39. As the body fails, death draws near.
40. Scintillation is perfect, that is, even terror is perfect.

Corollary.—It is not wrong to be afraid, but it is wrong to think that scintillation is terror.

41. Even those who avoid predators, sickness, and injury, will one day drop to the earth and never rise again.
42. The flight of the song is never ending.

About the author

Michael Cisco is an American writer, Deleuzian academic, and teacher.

Printed in Great Britain
by Amazon